PASSIONATE AWAKENING

PASSIONATE AWAKENING

Joy St. Clair

Chivers Press • G.K. Hall & Co.
Bath, England   Thorndike, Maine USA

IC KB MH VS LE ES PC DL MG

This Large Print edition is published by Chivers Press, England, and by
G.K. Hall & Co., USA.

Published in 1999 in the U.K. by arrangement with the author, care of
Laurence Pollinger.

Published in 1999 in the U.S. by arrangement with Laurence Pollinger,
Ltd.

U.K. Hardcover ISBN 0–7540–3635–9 (Chivers Large Print)
U.K. Softcover   ISBN 0–7540–3636–7 (Camden Large Print)
U.S. Softcover   ISBN 0–7838–8471–0 (Nightingale Series Edition)

The text of this Large Print edition is unabridged.
Other aspects of the book may vary from the original edition.

Set in 16 pt. New Times Roman.

Printed in Great Britain on acid-free paper.

British Library Cataloguing in Publication Data available

Library of Congress Cataloging-in-Publication Data

St. Clair, Joy.
    Passionate awakening / Joy St. Clair.
       p.   cm.
    ISBN 0–7838–8471–0 (lg. print : sc : alk. paper)
    1. Large type books.   I. Title.
  [PR6069.A4227P37   1999]
  823'.914—dc21   98–49002

CHAPTER ONE

'You're trespassing on private property.'

Felicity stared at the man in the black jogging suit who was blocking her way on the immaculate turf. His hair was a dark untamed cloud with a hint of the deepest chestnut so that with the sun behind him he appeared to wear a tawny halo.

There was a raw-boned leanness about his features which prevented him from being handsome in the conventional sense. Yet he was easily the most interesting-looking man she had seen for many a long day.

'This is not the public right-of-way, you know.' His voice was refined and his eyes were piercingly blue. He was mid-thirtyish, she supposed, and tall enough to be a basket-ball player.

A few yards behind him two women, leaning on croquet mallets, giggled.

Felicity gave him what she hoped was a friendly smile. She'd been driving all morning and just wanted to sit down with a cup of tea, not have to go back to the road and start all over again. 'I'm looking for The Old Smithy.' Tall chimneys visible through the trees indicated she was close. 'I thought I'd take the short cut instead of going all the way round.'

His eyes flicked over her trim, taller-than-average figure and she was conscious of the creases in her pink linen suit after her long journey.

'This is not a short cut.' His gaze dropped to her sensible low-heeled court shoes, ideal for driving. 'And your footwear is damaging my croquet lawn.'

She hastily stepped on to the gravelled verge. 'Sorry. I didn't realise.'

'What do you want with The Old Smithy?' he enquired. 'The place is empty. Has been for the past twelve months.'

'Yes, I know it's empty. I'm the new owner. My aunt . . .'

'Ah, I see. So Audrey was your aunt. You must be Miss Felicity Stafford. Why didn't you say so in the first place?'

'You didn't give me a chance.'

'Your Aunt Audrey spoke of you often,' he went on. 'You were her favourite niece. She thought so highly of you she bequeathed you her property.' He frowned. 'I suppose you had your own reasons for not setting foot in the place, to my knowledge, all the time she lived here.'

She resented the implication that she had neglected her aunt but couldn't blame him for thinking so. She'd have liked to visit but the old lady had always insisted on coming up to London instead—to see the bright lights and visit a show.

'You weren't even at the funeral,' he added.

How could she have attended? She had been visiting her brother in Canada at the time of her aunt's sudden demise.

Felicity felt at a disadvantage. 'Would you mind telling me who you are?'

Even as he replied she knew the answer. Lawson Quartermain, renowned bachelor playwright, owner of the ancient manor-house standing resplendently on the hill overlooking the grand sweep of lawns. Aunt Audrey had been on cordial terms with her neighbour and had conveyed an intriguing image of him. Charming when he liked, infuriating when he liked, worshipped by actresses young and old.

' . . . And my name is Quartermain,' he was confirming. 'I promised the solicitors I'd keep an eye on The Old Smithy while it stood empty.'

It was decent of him to take the trouble to check on unauthorised callers, she thought—a true neighbourhood-watch gesture—but she could not find it in her heart to say so, not while his dark brows were meeting like that.

The all-enquiring gaze moved first to her hazel eyes and then to her short springy curls, the colour of caramel. 'You're very like your aunt.'

'So I've been told.' She ferreted in her tote-bag and produced the door keys, to show him she meant business. 'I've left my car outside the main gates. My aunt said there was a short cut to the house, a path to save having to go round. May I use it?'

'Be my guest. It's the other side of the kissing-gate.' He pointed to a little swing gate close to the hedge, almost hidden by an overhanging willow tree. 'I imagine you'll be selling the place. It's a bit of a millstone for a young person such as yourself.'

That had been her intention. Sell it and buy something more manageable, more suitable for two young children. 'Why no. Not immediately anyhow.'

She couldn't imagine why she had said that. Perhaps it was the way he presumed to know her plans that made her want to contradict him.

She rattled the keys blithely. 'I shall definitely be moving in. As you pointed out, it's my first visit to Upton St Jude, but I think it's a lovely little town.'

'You know your own business best.' He glanced at his watch. 'Well, I'll bid you good afternoon, Miss Stafford. I have a lot to do.'

She stared after his retreating figure. Nothing like being made to feel welcome!

At the kissing-gate she was compelled to glance back to watch him stride across the lawn to join the two women.

With their scarves and bangles and flawlessly made-up faces, both could be taken for actresses. The younger of the two had blonde hair reaching half-way down her back and her white T-shirt and jeans were skin-tight

4

showing off a minuscule waist. There was something familiar about her and Felicity recognised Kiki Dawn, the new acting discovery, currently the talk of the London theatre circuit.

She didn't know the other woman, who was the wrong side of forty but well preserved. In a red flying-suit her black hair worn in a stylish chignon, she cut a striking figure.

Felicity made her way under the willows and along the overgrown path until the former smithy came into view, a squat dwelling with red-brick walls and latticed windows. The paint was peeling here and there but it was to be expected after being empty for so long.

Her aunt had told her that the Quartermain family had once owned the entire estate which had originally stretched for miles and included several villages, but over the centuries pieces had been sold off to pay debts. Death duties had dealt the final blow and they had sold up completely over a hundred years ago.

The outbuildings had been disposed of separately, the lodge being made into two flats, the stables and smithy turned into dwelling-houses.

The manor itself had stood empty for nearly a century until Quartermain had bought it. He was gradually restoring it to its former glory, but full restoration was expected to take many years.

Inside The Old Smithy all was still and

silent. Leading from the sombre hall was a living-room, a sitting-room and a decent-sized cloakroom, as well as a kitchen and lavatory. Everywhere the wallpaper and furnishings were from a bygone age and a smell of muskiness pervaded the property.

Felicity tried the tap in the kitchen. The pipes made an ominous clanging noise and the water trickled rustily at first then gushed clear. The gas had been turned off but she forayed among the cobwebs under the stairs to find the mains and turn it on again. She rinsed out the heavy iron kettle and placed it on the antiquated stove. Having had the foresight to bring a tea-bag and an individual triangle of milk she soon had her longed-for cup of tea.

She carried the cup through to the living-room and sank thankfully on to an ancient couch which had sheets and blankets piled at one end as if it had been used as a bed.

Aunt Audrey had developed a heart condition in later years and had probably shut the upper rooms off to avoid having to climb the stairs. The last nine months of her life had been spent in a nursing home at Bath, where Felicity had visited her, and her last will and testament had taken three months to settle, so the state of the place came as no surprise.

Felicity recalled her aunt with affection. Back in her twenties she had spent a holiday in Upton St Jude and there she had met Charles, her one and only love. They had lived at The

Old Smithy all their married life but, sadly, Charles died just before he was due to retire and Audrey had gone on for another twenty years alone. 'I've had a wonderful life,' the old lady used to say, 'I found my destiny here'.

Her cup drained, Felicity got up and walked about the room, tapping the walls and looking for signs of dry rot, thankful to discover that the place seemed to be structurally sound. At least that was something.

There was a huge fireplace which must have been part of the original forge. Felicity could just picture it cleaned up, with horse-brasses hanging on its brickwork and a blazing log fire roaring up its wide chimney.

Between the living-room and sitting-room were double connecting doors, every crevice sealed with draught-excluder. As she stripped the rotting fabric away and opened the doors her fertile imagination conjured up a long table down the centre, complete with lace cloth, gleaming silver, sparkling glassware and bowls of flowers.

'It will look nice when I throw a dinner party,' she murmured. Then she laughed. Today was the first time she had even considered living here. But now she had the idea she couldn't let it go.

She ascended the stairs to the top landing, a gloomy nook-and-cranny sort of place with little steps going up and down. In the rooms the fireplaces were made of marble and there were plaster roses on the ceilings, but the dust was thick and the furniture sparse. It looked as if she had been right about Aunt Audrey not using this part of the house.

She could make the master bedroom her own, Felicity thought, her heart warming to the prospect. It had dimity curtains at present and smelt of stale lavender water but she could already visualise pastel velvets and delicate nets, and detect the scent of potpourri.

The two rooms at the rear would do nicely for Troy and Bryony. And the little boxroom could be converted into a bathroom. She'd paint it yellow to catch the morning sun.

Downstairs again she saw the hall floor was covered with black and white tiles. They were dingy at the moment but not beyond redemption. And the cloakroom would be ideal for her easel and drawing-board, although she would probably have to build a shed in the garden for use as a carpentry workshop.

Ever since leaving college she had designed furniture for a London manufacturer. When she had informed them she must leave to look after the children they had suggested she work from home on a new mail-order line involving easily assembled occasional furniture kits such as coffee-tables and flower tubs. She had jumped at the chance.

So it didn't matter where she lived. As the children, currently living in Hertfordshire, would have to go to a new school whether she chose London or Sussex, it would be no more of an upheaval for them than if she stuck to her original plans.

She was sure Crispin would agree to her change of direction. Her brother-in-law was always so adaptable and grateful for everything she did to help.

When she'd first offered to foster his motherless children, he'd been hesitant but she'd convinced him it would work. Ever since Trish had died they had been in the hands of various minders and were rapidly getting out of control. They needed a stable upbringing and who better to look after them than their mother's sister?

She had intended remaining in London, where she'd lived all her life, and getting a larger flat for her and the children. But this new challenge appealed to her. She was twenty-four, an age to be adventurous. It was now or never.

Besides, Crispin spent most of his working-life abroad. He would love coming to this house to unwind. It was in a rural area on the south coast, with easy access to the sea and so restful, he would go back to the Gulf rejuvenated.

She walked dreamily to the window, wondering what madness possessed her. She wasn't usually quite so impulsive and it excited her. Outside was a cherry-tree in full flower, its

9

blossom showering like snow onto the overgrown lawn. Its beauty took her breath away and she knew she was making the right decision.

A tour of the weed-tangled garden brought her to the open door of a tumbledown garage filled with worm-eaten gardening implements. A large black cat was curled up in a wheel-barrow. It got up and made a fuss of her, weaving around her legs and rubbing its head against her shoes.

'Thanks,' she said, 'it's nice to get a welcome from somebody around here.'

Beside the garage she discovered a gravelled drive-way leading to the main road which would in future avoid the necessity for crossing her neighbour's land to gain entry to the house.

Today however she'd left her car outside the main entrance to the estate and was forced to walk back the way she had come. As she ducked under the willows and sidled through the kissing-gate, she wondered if she would bump into Lawson Quartermain again. He was busy, he'd said, so he would most likely have finished his game of croquet and gone indoors. She didn't know whether to be pleased or sorry.

She had reached her car when she saw him, perched on the top of a five-barred gate as if he had been waiting for her.

'Well, have you decided to stay?' he asked without preamble.

She nodded. 'Yes. I shall definitely be staying.'

He regarded her pensively. 'Are you sure you've thought it through? After London you may find Upton a bit of a backwater. And you'd feel out of place on the estate. The residents here are mostly elderly . . .'

'Anyone would think you didn't want me to stay!'

'It makes no difference to me,' he replied evenly. 'I'm thinking of you . . .'

'Well, I think I shall like it here. I just have to consult . . . someone to see if he has any objection.'

'Fiancé?'

'No, I'm not engaged.'

A smile slanted his lips. 'A pretty girl like you?'

To her annoyance, she blushed. If only he knew! She came from a large happy family, now scattered across the world, and had looked forward to marriage and children but, although she'd had plenty of menfriends, had never met anyone who remotely resembled her ideal.

'You're too fussy,' her mother had told her. But she didn't see why she should marry just to prove she could. And she was quite content with her unmarried state. She made her own decisions and answered to no one.

'I thought young women married young these days,' said Quartermain.

'Not this one. I'm a career girl. I doubt if I

11

shall be getting married.'

He gave a grunt. 'Perhaps it's just as well if you intend living here. Marriage means squalling babies and rampaging youngsters. The neighbours are mostly old and wouldn't relish the noise. Neither would I. I like peace and quiet while I write.'

He sounded pompous and she controlled an impulse to argue. She thought of the children and recalled a half-forgotten clause in the freehold which decreed that the current owner of the manor must always recommend any other property owners on the estate. It was to ensure compatibility between neighbours in this enclosed community. She decided to keep quiet about Troy and Bryony. 'So you'll recommend me?'

He looked puzzled for a moment, as if he too had forgotten. Then, 'I shall not hesitate to recommend you, Miss Stafford. You have my word.'

She smiled guiltily. 'Thank you very much, Mr Quartermain.'

She turned to unlock the car door then glanced back at him, catching him in an unguarded moment and detecting a spark of warmth in his hitherto indifferent appraisal. It was so unexpected she experienced a quickening of her heartbeat and swallowed hard. A moment later his expression was bland again and she decided she had imagined it. She was angry with herself then for allowing his physical presence to send her senses haywire.

'I don't suppose we shall be seeing much of each other, Miss Stafford,' he intoned drily. 'As I said, I'm a busy man and I go up to town quite a lot. But I wish you all the best in your new home.'

'Thank you.' She couldn't resist adding, 'Where I come from newcomers are greeted with a pot of tea.'

He threw back his head and laughed scornfully. 'That's all very well for people who have nothing better to do. As for tea, it's the world's worst time-waster.'

She had an idea he was teasing her but couldn't be sure. Quickly she slid into the driving-seat, reversed the car and drove off before he could make any more fatuous remarks.

Presently, out on the London road, she was struck by the funny side of the situation. What would he say when he learned there would be two children living with her at The Old Smithy? Two children who had lost their mother and been allowed to run wild? By the time he found out he would have signed the recommendation and it would be too late for him to do anything about it. Served him right, she thought gleefully.

*   *   *

Felicity spent several weekends working on the

house. Plumbers and electricians came and went. Her furniture was brought from London and she scoured the local second-hand showrooms. She and Crispin were sharing the expenses but there was no need to be extravagant. She had already made furniture for the children's rooms and in time would be making more.

At the end of June, when carpets had been laid and curtains hung, she moved in. Then she invited Crispin, on a flying visit from the Gulf, to come and make his inspection.

'You've done wonders!' he exclaimed, trailing her from the green and plum sitting-room into the gold and brown living-room. 'This is like going from midsummer to autumn.'

'I'm glad you noticed. That was my intention.'

The black cat she had found in the garage that first day was disappearing out of the window.

'That's Pi. He goes with the house.' She added, 'The neighbour who's been feeding him since Aunt Audrey died says he sneaks off to the manor at regular intervals. Off there now I shouldn't wonder. We have a traitor in the camp.'

'Never mind, the kids will love him.'

In the newly fitted kitchen, cheerfully decorated in cream and emerald, she plugged in the electric kettle to make a pot of tea.

Crispin carried the tray out to the sunny patio where a rainbow assortment of painted chairs were clustered around a sunshade-topped table.

'Are you really sure about this, Felicity, dear?' He sipped the refreshing brew. 'It's not easy bringing up children at the best of times and my two have become proper little monsters. It's not too late to change your mind. I won't think any less of you.'

'Yes, I'm sure. I want them. They know me. Even when Trish was alive I always took them off your hands whenever you two wanted a break. It's the ideal solution. And it's a lovely area. There's a stream running between our land and Quartermain's. And Upton St Jude is a pretty town with a beach and a little harbour.'

They exchanged affectionate smiles. Each was very fond of the other, but there was nothing romantic about their relationship. Felicity had only ever seen Crispin as 'family', her brother-in-law, father of Troy and Bryony. He looked on her as a good friend. In any case, she reasoned, Trish had been so radiant, it wasn't likely he would fall for her very ordinary sister.

'I can't tell you how grateful I am, Felicity,' he murmured. 'When Trish ... died I just didn't know which way to turn. But you've been wonderful, calling regularly to see them, taking them out at weekends. And now this . . .' As his voice broke, he got to his feet and walked across the lawn to stand under the cherry tree, now in full leaf.

Felicity regarded the back of his fair head. Dear Crispin! He was tall and elegantly slim, what her mother considered a perfect catch. With his soft grey eyes and lightly freckled nose, he appeared boyishly vulnerable, even at thirty-two. Trish had mothered him along with the two children. He had simply gone to pieces after her untimely death in an influenza epidemic.

Tenderly, Felicity recalled her beautiful sister—a happy-go-lucky person, full of the joy of living and everyone's idea of a glamorous blonde. She had been the image of their vivacious mother, whereas Felicity favoured good old dependable Dad.

Felicity knew she was the best person to foster the children. Her parents had both retired and lived in Spain. Her brothers and sister were wed and had families of their own. She was the youngest of the Staffords, with no ties, and she couldn't let Troy and Bryony be messed about by strangers any longer. They would be her ready-made family.

She and Crispin had worked out the arrangements—he would support the children, but because he was employed by an oil company and worked in their overseas office, their care and upbringing would be left entirely to her. It really was the best of both worlds.

She could be their foster-mother while still working at the occupation she loved, her carpentry.

Joining Crispin beneath the tree, she invited, 'Come and see my workshop.'

She showed him the new shed where she had installed her bench and carpentry tools. After each design was blue-printed it was imperative that it worked in practice and a sample of the finished product had to be sent to her employers. She liked nothing better than to be up to her ankles in wood shavings.

'Will you be collecting the children directly the school term finishes in July?' he asked as they went along the path in the direction of the kissing-gate.

She nodded.

His expression clouded. 'I wish I could be here when they move in, especially when they see their new bedrooms. You've been so ingenious.' He hunched his shoulders in a helpless way that wrung her heart. 'But the oil business is ever-pressing. Perhaps I should get a transfer to a position nearer home . . .'

'You mustn't give it a thought,' she protested. 'I can manage perfectly well. You know you love the life.'

He brightened. 'Bless you, Felicity. And thank you.' He took her hands and drew her towards him to plant a kiss on her forehead. 'For everything.'

A dry branch snapped beside them and she

17

twisted her head to see Quartermain observing them, blue eyes hostile.

'Excuse me.' He spoke with studied politeness. 'Sorry to disturb you, but there's a phone call for you, Miss Stafford, at the manor.'

'Oh! Thank you.' She stood back from Crispin's embrace. 'I'm sorry to have inconvenienced you, Mr Quartermain.'

'I'll be off then,' said Crispin. 'Goodbye, Felicity, my dear. I'll be in touch.'

Lawson Quartermain watched them for a moment then politely retreated out of earshot.

'So!' Crispin turned down the corners of his mouth. 'That's your neighbour. I see what you meant when you said he was intimidating. You'd better get your phone connected soon. He won't like playing errand-boy.'

'Telecom promised it by next week.'

She waved him goodbye then went through the gate to where Quartermain was waiting for her, sitting in a kind of golf trolley.

'Climb aboard,' he invited ungraciously.

CHAPTER TWO

Felicity was unable to see where she was to sit in the strange little vehicle which only had seating for one.

'You'll have to stand on the bar at the back,'

said Quartermain with a malicious gleam in his eye, 'and hold on to my shoulders.'

'No thanks. I'll walk, if you don't mind.'

'I do mind! Don't be silly!' he snapped. 'Your mother's holding on from Spain. Stop being so selfish and think how much the call's costing her.'

He might have said so in the first place, she thought, biting her tongue on a caustic reply. As she climbed on the bar she was thankful she was wearing jeans. He drove carefully up the slope and she never came close to falling off, but she felt decidedly odd perched there with her hands firmly clamped on his broad cashmered shoulders and the smell of his aftershave, musky and expensive, prickling her nostrils.

Up close the manor house looked impressive. It was one of those ancient stone buildings with deeply-recessed windows and invincible-looking walls. There was even a tower at one end. Curtains hung at the downstairs windows but most of the upper rooms appeared unlived in.

The trolley travelled through a gateway leading to the rear of the house and halted in a large courtyard. When Felicity had climbed down, Quartermain said curtly, 'This way.'

He led her over the cobbles and ushered her indoors to a study where the phone lay off the hook. Then he made himself scarce.

Her mother was ringing to find out how the

move had gone. Mrs Stafford had remembered Aunt Audrey saying the manor belonged to a Lawson Quartermain and she had got the number from directory enquiries.

'Could you wait till I get my own phone connected before you ring again, Mum?' Felicity pleaded. 'My neighbour is not the easiest of people to get along with.'

'Really?' Her mother sounded incredulous. 'He was positively charming to me.'

He would be, thought Felicity wryly.

She finished the call and looked round the study. It was delightfully untidy with papers cluttering the desk and textbooks scattered over the carpet. She supposed this was where Quartermain worked and was suitably awestruck.

She heard a mewing sound and turned to see Pi lying flat out in a pool of sunshine under the window. 'Traitor!' she hissed.

She was squinting down at a sheet of paper in the typewriter when she heard someone approaching. Thinking it was Quartermain, she swung round guiltily. But it was a tall angular woman, about fifty, with a boney face and shrewd eyes. She wore a floral overall and a green felt hat rammed over grey hair.

'Oh, beg pardon,' she said, plonking a tray on the desk, 'I just came to collect the teacups.' She paused and seemed to be trying to gauge whether Felicity was a visitor of importance or not. 'I'm Win Pilgrim, the housekeeper.'

20

'Felicity Stafford.' She grinned. 'I'm nobody.'

'Stafford? You must be Audrey's niece. I was so sorry to hear of her death. She was a nice old lady.' Win was filling the tray with teacups gleaned from the desk, the bookshelf, the window ledge and the floor.

'I thought he didn't drink tea.'

'Doesn't drink tea?' A laugh erupted in the housekeeper's throat. 'That's a good one. He never stops.'

The laugh was infectious and Felicity joined in, deciding she liked the woman.

Win delved behind the curtains for more cups. 'Hello! Is he waiting out there for you?'

'Yes.' Felicity followed the other's gaze. Quartermain was leaning against the trolley, drumming his fingers on the bodywork, his thick brows almost meeting—as usual. 'He looks annoyed.'

'Take no notice,' said Win blithely. 'I don't. His bark's worse than his bite.'

'I'd better go all the same.'

Lawson straightened as Felicity walked towards the trolley.

'I'm sorry to have troubled you,' she said. 'If you'd told me it was my mother I wouldn't have argued about riding on the bar.' His accusation about her selfishness still rankled. She decided to get it all off her chest. 'And I didn't neglect my aunt, you know. She preferred to visit me in London. And I was in

21

Canada when she died so I couldn't attend her funeral.'

'You seem to have covered everything, Miss Stafford,' he answered sardonically. 'Get in! I'll run you back.'

'Oh, no! I've messed you about too much already. You'll be wanting to work. I'll walk home.'

'Don't be silly.' He made her feel like a tedious schoolgirl. 'My concentration has already been broken.'

His remark cut the conversation dead and she meekly climbed on the bar.

He dropped her beside the kissing-gate.

'Thanks. I'm going to have the phone connected but there's a short delay . . .'

'So you gave my number.'

'No, I did not!' she cried. 'Mother discovered it for herself.' She added haughtily, 'Don't worry. I've told her not to ring me through you again. On pain of death.'

She expected a smile but his blue eyes watched her steadily. 'That was a touching scene I witnessed earlier. I thought you told me you weren't engaged.'

'Crispin is my brother-in-law.'

'I see!'

She didn't like the way he said that. There was a tinge of scorn in the glance he trained on her now and she felt uncomfortable. However she refused to go on explaining things to him. Let him think what he liked. 'It's none of your business!'

'I thought we agreed it was my business.' With that he turned the trolley round and headed back towards the manor.

Her eyes followed the curious vehicle's progress up the steep slope. Just before it reached the top, a taxi swept in through the iron gates. It stopped beside the trolley and a woman alighted. It was the older, black-haired woman who had been playing croquet.

In a flash her name came back to Felicity— Vera Valance, once famous dramatic actress, a favourite of her mother's in fact, but now considered a bit of a has-been.

As Quartermain clambered out of the trolley the woman threw her arms round his shoulders and kissed his cheek.

He disentangled himself from her embrace and dug in his pockets to pay off the taxi, then the woman climbed on to the back of the trolley and together they rode the rest of the way to the manor.

Felicity turned away, strangely disturbed by the scene she had witnessed.

*   *   *

'Well, what do you think of it?' asked Felicity.

The Old Smithy nestled sleepily in the sun as they stood before it, but its rustic charm appeared lost on the children.

She'd fetched them from Hertfordshire and

knew they were tired. During the journey, watching them in the back of the car by means of the rear-view mirror she had seen little Bryony slumped disconsolately on the seat, her thumb in her mouth, her other hand clutching a rag doll, while Troy sat stiff and awkward staring out of the window, his blue eyes devoid of emotion.

No matter what bright remark she had made to them it had been met with a monosyllabic reply.

She led the way into the hall. 'Well?' she asked again.

'S'all right, I suppose,' Troy conceded.

He didn't smile and Felicity sensed he was hard-pressed not to cry.

Bryony had no such inhibitions about showing her feelings. Tears gathered in her eyes as she twisted a hank of her blonde hair. 'Don't like it. Want to go back to Miss Jackson.'

Poor kids! They'd been pushed from pillar to post this last year since Trish had died. Was it any wonder they were prepared to treat any new prospect with suspicion?

'No you don't, Bry,' said Troy fiercely. 'Old Jackers is the pits . . .'

'Troy!' exclaimed Felicity, shocked.

He looked balefully at her. 'She is! She wears iron knickers and smells of nasty ointment.'

Bryony removed her thumb from her
24

mouth. 'She does, Auntie Fliss. She rubs it on her knee.'

Felicity knew all about their recent minder, a sporty Amazon who wore a surgical corset and had a torn cartilage after injuring herself on the ladies' football field.

'Forget about Miss Jackson,' she said, 'You're living here now.'

'For ever?' asked Troy dubiously.

'If you want to.' She put a hand to his shining blond head but he dodged away from her.

'You'll get married,' he accused.

'No, I won't. Honestly. I shall be here for you as long as you need me. I promise.'

He regarded her solemnly then turned away and mounted the stairs, followed by his sister.

Felicity held her breath as they reached the door of Troy's room. She had endeavoured to make it suitable for a boy of seven and it had taken all her ingenuity to come up with a pirate theme. She had made most of the fixtures herself and Crispin had paid for the materials. The high bed was shaped like a fo'c's'le from which flew the skull-and-crossbones; the wall bore a hand-painted treasure-island map; the dressing-table was a sea chest; the chairs were sawn-off barrels and there were various brass fitting from old ships which she had gleaned from second-hand shops. He showed a moment's surprised interest then the shutters went up on his

25

expression.

'Yes, it's very nice.'

She wanted to hug him and tell him everything would be all right, but sensed he would be embarrassed. He had taken it upon himself to protect his sister and must be worn out with the responsibility, young as he was. He was being very brave but the least thing was likely to start a flood.

They went along to Bryony's room, decorated in pink and white stripes like a stick of peppermint rock. The bed was a fairy coach with gauzy drapes, pulled by life-size ponies which Felicity had cut out with a jigsaw and painted. There were mobiles of frogs and princes, a pumpkin pouffe and a 'magic' lamp on the dressing-table.

The six-year-old girl burst into tears and threw herself on to the bed. 'Don't want it. Want to go home. Want Mummy!'

Troy sat down beside her and stroked her hair. 'Don't go on so, Bry. Auntie Fliss is trying to help. Daddy said we've got to give her a chance.'

Felicity went out and shut the door. She only hoped she'd done the right thing. A meal might help.

Downstairs she set about preparing beefburgers, cake and milk shakes.

She had hoped Pi would be around to welcome the children but he was nowhere to be found. Trust him, just when she needed

26

him. Probably lording it up at the manor, she thought resentfully.

Presently they sat down together at the kitchen table.

The children were very much alike, thought Felicity, watching them toying with their food. Having two fair-haired parents, both were platinum blond. They favoured Trish in looks and had inherited Crispin's light smattering of freckles. But they were too thin and Troy especially seemed to be all elbows and knees.

'Do try to finish your cake,' she coaxed them. 'Daddy will be so pleased if you put on some weight.'

But Bryony's lids were already drooping and she pushed her plate away.

As Troy yawned, Felicity said, 'Bedtime, I think. You'll feel better after a good night's sleep. Tomorrow we can go exploring.'

She carried Bryony up the stairs and, dispensing with washing and brushing teeth just this once, eased her out of her clothes and into her pyjamas. By the time the child's head touched the pillow she was asleep, still clutching the rag doll which went by the name of Maggie-Ann and had been given to her by her mother.

Felicity kissed her niece's forehead and went along the landing to see how Troy was getting on.

He'd put a barrel-chair in front of his door and when he removed it she discovered he was already in his pyjamas.

'I didn't want you to see me,' he muttered. 'Old Jackers used to come in without knocking.'

Felicity hid a smile and tucked the sheets round him. She bent to kiss him but he turned his head to the wall and only grunted when she wished him 'goodnight'.

In the morning she was alarmed when she went into Bryony's room and found it empty. Hearing murmuring next door she rushed in to see two humps in the bed.

Troy surfaced. 'She was crying. She didn't like being in that strange bed . . .'

Felicity felt a pang of sympathy, remembering her own childhood holidays, spent visiting countless relations and sleeping in an assortment of beds. 'That's all right.' She uncovered the girl's golden head. 'Would you like a night light?'

Bryony nodded.

Troy sat up. 'You won't smack her, will you?'

'Smack her? Why should I?'

'She . . . had an accident.'

Felicity was out of her depth. 'Accident?'

Bryony let out a wail. 'You promised you wouldn't tell.' And she pummelled her brother's chest.

'She'll find out,' said Troy, 'When she goes to make your bed.'

'Oh, I see.' Felicity made a mental note to

buy a waterproof sheet. 'Stop worrying, lovey. I shan't make a fuss. Accidents happen.'

'A big black cat came on my bed in the night,' said Troy. 'Is he ours?'

'Yes, that's Pi. I wondered where he'd got to.'

'A cat?' asked Bryony brightening for the first time. 'Oh goody!'

Felicity had thought that during the summer holidays the two of them would play happily in the garden while she concentrated on her work, and she planned to take them out at weekends. She soon learned she was being too optimistic. They wouldn't stay in the garden and made nuisances of themselves among the other residents.

One by one irate neighbours came to complain about the latest escapades. They had dug holes in the Foresters' garden at The Lodge, 'terrorised' the dog belonging to old Mrs Barnes at the converted stables, 'stolen' the parson's notes for the milkman, upturned elderly Miss Keen's dustbin, broken branches and generally run amok.

Felicity seemed to spend all her time apologising. She understood how annoying it must be for the other residents and realised she would have to keep her eye on them all the time.

One person who did not complain was Lawson Quartermain and she couldn't believe her good fortune. Then she heard from Win

Pilgrim that he was away in London and that explained it. Just as well, she thought. She wanted them to be a bit more civilised before he found out about them.

She decided to treat them to a morning on the beach. She was just thinking she had found the answer to her problem when she heard angry shouting and saw them throwing the pebbles about, much to the annoyance of the countless sunbathers.

A short drive brought them to a little cove, but here they kicked other children's sand-castles over. Taking them home, Felicity grumbled, 'Can't you be trusted anywhere?'

'Sorry,' they chorused, 'We didn't mean it.'

She knew it was true. They didn't mean it, they were just wild and thoughtless. But sometimes she wondered if she had been crazy, anticipating she could cope with two boisterous, demanding children.

She was tired. Working during the night after the little darlings were in bed was taking its toll of her energy. It would be all right, she told herself, after they started school in September.

On the credit side she and the children loved the old house with its nooks and crannies and dark places.

'Is it haunted?' asked Troy.

'No, of course not.'

He looked disappointed. 'What rotten luck!'

Felicity laughed.

'There might be a ghost,' he persisted. 'Can we explore the attic and find out?'

'If you like, but don't start scaring each other.'

They trotted off and she got down to some work. She had transformed the cloakroom into a drawing-office to accommodate her easel, high stool and filing-cabinets. Designing the mail-order kits was absorbing and she was currently working on a set of occasional tables. She had just started on a complicated mediaeval pattern, when she realised how quiet the house was.

She scrambled up the attic ladder and pushed open the trapdoor to see the children sitting on the floor playing Snakes and Ladders, surrounded by bric-à-brac. Caught in a beam of sunshine from the dormer window, their hair turned into golden haloes, they looked like angels.

'There's a lot of stuff up here. I really must clear it out,' remarked Felicity, picking up a couple of handbags. 'These, for instance, could go to Oxfam.'

She tackled the job the following afternoon while the children were playing in the garden with strict instructions not to roam. Periodically she glanced through the window to check that they were behaving themselves.

It was a dusty business but soon she had six plastic dustbin sacks filled. The handbags were of good quality leather and bore the lingering smell of old face powder. At once the image of her aunt came to mind and she remembered how she used to talk about finding her destiny in this place.

Felicity leaned on the window sill and gazed out over the trees wondering if she would find her own destiny here.

In her heart of hearts she wanted to keep the children with her for as long as was possible, until they married even, or went off to college. That was her destiny. She was equally aware that if ever Crispin decided to marry again she would lose them. It was a possibility on which she usually preferred not to dwell. She had to admit her position was precarious. Unless . . . She took a shuddering breath. Unless he married her!

But she had already established she wasn't his type of woman. Trish had been a classic glamorous blonde, which she most definitely was not. Looks may be skin deep but men stuck to the same ideal. And it wasn't just her colouring that was wrong, it was her whole mental attitude.

All the same, she and Crispin got on well together. She liked him—a lot. She could learn to love him given time. And he her. Perhaps she did love him. What was love after all? A liking, a mutual respect, interest in the same things? They had that already. Marriage to Crispin would solve everything. The children would be hers forever.

She didn't know how long she stood there leaning on the sill, but was jolted out of her meditations by the sight of Lawson Quartermain driving the golf trolley across the manor lawns and heading straight for the kissing–gate.

She anxiously scanned the garden to see what the children were up to. She hadn't planned on him meeting them just yet. She had hoped to find an opportunity to tell him about them first and so clear her conscience. If he saw them now there was no telling what he would think.

Bryony was kneeling by the hedge making mud pies and Troy was swinging from a branch of a willow tree directly above her. At that moment the branch snapped and he fell among the pies. Bryony set up a caterwauling and began pelting him with mud. He retaliated spiritedly.

The golf trolley had stopped beside the kissing gate and Quartermain had alighted. He bent over to remove something which had been on the floor between his feet and she saw it was a tray laden with a silver tea service, a vacuum flask and china cups and saucers.

As sedately as a butler he carried it towards the gate just as the children surged along the path, whooping and hurling the mud as they went.

'Oh no!' wailed Felicity barely able to look. The dramatist and the children were on a collision course. She tried to open the window to shout a warning but the catch was old and rusty and would not budge.

She dashed down the ladder and stairs, knowing she was too late. As she sped across the garden there came an ear-splitting crash. She rounded the hedge to see tea-bags, sugar cubes and chocolate biscuits everywhere. The teapot lay in the ditch, the milk jug had emptied its contents over Quartermain's jeans and suede shoes—handmade by the look of them—and the china cups and saucers lay in shattered pieces over a wide area.

She restrained an impulse to laugh and waited for him to speak.

His tone was dry as dust. 'Where you come from people bring newcomers a tray of tea, I believe.'

'So that's what you were doing!'

'Belatedly, yes.'

'Oh dear, I'm so sorry for what happened. Troy! Bryony!' She yanked them to her. 'Apologise to this gentleman at once!'

Eyes downcast, they mumbled something as Quartermain watched them disdainfully.

'I assume these are not your offspring, Miss Stafford?'

'No, they're my sister's. Crispin's their father.'

'That's a relief.' He watched her suspiciously.

'You will make me very happy if you tell me

34

they are only here on a flying visit and will be returning whence they came this very day.' He paused. 'You will tell me that, won't you?'

Bryony took her thumb from her mouth and smiled up at him. 'Me and Troy live here.'

He stared deliberately at Felicity. 'Is this true?'

'Course it is,' put in Troy.

'Yes, it's true,' she confessed, 'I meant to tell you but you were away and . . . and . . .'

His eyes called her a liar.

'I'm sorry,' she murmured.

'So you should be.' He sounded like a schoolmaster reprimanding a naughty child. 'You deceived me, Miss Stafford. You deliberately omitted to mention two children would be living here with you. And such undisciplined children at that. Didn't you?'

Her patience deserted her. 'Yes! Do you really blame me? It was quite plain you're a child-hater!' She thought she saw an expression of pain cross his features but it was gone in a flash. 'For heaven's sake! They need time to settle in. My sister died last year and they're very young to be motherless. They've been through a great deal recently.'

'I have the other residents to consider,' he rejoined. 'I shall expect you to keep these two under control.'

'I intend to!' she exploded. 'Give me a chance!'

'Very well.' He regarded her levelly. 'But if

35

there is any trouble I shall have no alternative but to take redress through the courts.'

'Wh . . . what? You're not serious!'

'Try me!'

'But they're only children. Aren't you being a little hard on them? Where's your sense of humour?'

'I've said all I'm going to say. Good day, Miss Stafford.' He swivelled on his heel and walked back to the golf trolley.

Overcome with frustration, Felicity turned on the children. 'You were very naughty, both of you! I shall have to punish you.' She thought for a moment. 'No television today!'

They raised a chorus of protests.

'I wanna see the bears!'

'I wanna see Mickey Mouse!'

'No television!' she repeated firmly. 'You've got to understand you can't go round upsetting people.'

She retrieved the silver teapot and the broken flask which must have contained hot water. Oh dear! In great style, he had been bringing her that welcoming cup of tea she had taunted him about, and all he had got for his trouble was soggy jeans.

There was a dent in the teapot and she took it to the shed to try and straighten it with a wooden mallet but only made things worse. She would have to get it repaired by a silversmith.

For a tantalising moment she speculated on

36

what might have happened had Quartermain found her alone and they had shared a pot of tea, getting to know each other, becoming friends.

She shook the fantasy away. They would have found something else to argue over most likely. Right from their first meeting he had gone out of his way to snipe at her. And she couldn't forget how he had tried to talk her out of moving in. It was baffling. She usually got on well with people, but Lawson Quartermain was a man apart.

CHAPTER THREE

The winter term started at the children's new school in Upton St Jude and at last Felicity had time to herself. Her work had been piling up and she realised she was going to be hard-pressed to meet her deadline for a matching set of turntable bookcases and video-cases. She was experimenting on these particular items, using marquetry panels of light and dark wood, and the end product promised to be exciting.

Her boss made several anxious phone calls but she managed to stall him while she worked late into the night. The items were finally dispatched a week late and, for the first time in her professional career, she received a mild reprimand.

She enjoyed creating original concepts and much of her time was taken up browsing through books and visiting stately homes for ideas and inspiration. Dozens of notebooks had been filled with sketches of grasses, flowers, shells, fish skeletons, even parts of watches which could be used for decoration purposes.

She could not remember a time when she had not been in love with wood and it had come as no surprise to her family when she decided to study design at college. An added bonus had been the discovery that she had a flair for carpentry too. For her eighteenth birthday her parents had bought her an electric drill and a work-bench with all the gadgets but some of the more delicate work she preferred to do manually, using old-fashioned tools and methods handed down through generations by master craftsmen.

Furniture design went hand in hand with soft furnishings and she had also taken a course in needlework and embroidery while still at college. Though she said it herself, she was good at it.

In the back attic of her mind was a yearning to be independent of the firm for which she worked. They were an old-established concern and inclined to be cautious when it came to new ideas. If she had her own company she could experiment to her heart's content.

The dreams she had! Her designs would be exclusive and she kept a separate sketch book crammed with her more adventurous ideas, most of them probably too outlandish cover to become reality. On the one and only occasion she had offered her employers a futuristic design they had politely refused it and advised her to stick to tradition.

For the moment she was content with doing her job to the best of her ability and giving value for money. Starting up on her own would take time, something she did not have in abundance right now.

However, she did find time to take the silver teapot in for repair. It was ready for her collection in the middle of October and she examined it critically. They'd made a brave attempt at disguising the dent but it would never be quite the same again.

On a mild autumnal afternoon, when the lanes were dredged with yellow and brown leaves, and a smell of bonfires filled the air, she donned her hand-made 'Navaho' cape and her leather boots and trudged over to the manor to return the teapot to its owner.

She took the long way round, past the stream, marvelling at the colours of the trees and listening to the birdsong. After living for so long in London, it had taken her some time to get used to the quietness and tranquillity of the countryside but now she loved it and couldn't imagine ever wanting to live in a city again. And it was certainly the best place to bring up children. The good clean air seemed to give them an appetite and they were both filling out nicely.

Two gardeners were working on the manor rockery and they called a greeting to her as she passed. In the rear courtyard was a garage, its doors open to reveal the golf trolley, plus a sleek white Lotus Turbo and a Land-Rover, the latter being washed down by a young lad. It occurred to her that a place this large would need plenty of staff to keep it going.

She continued to the house. Through the study window she saw Quartermain seated at his typewriter, chin in hand, staring into space.

For a moment she hesitated, unwilling to be guilty of interrupting his train of thought yet again. Perhaps if she went further along the cobbled way she would come to the kitchen and find Win Pilgrim. She was creeping stealthily past when Quartermain looked up and saw her. At once he bounded to his feet.

A moment later the door opened and he appeared, dressed in an old fisherman's jersey and grey flannels, his feet pushed into a pair of rope sandals. Very Bohemian, she thought. She sensed an air of melancholy about him and realised the business of writing plays must be a lonely occupation.

She took the teapot from her carrier-bag and waved it at him. 'I've come to return your property and to apologise once more for myself and the children,' she said with a rush. 'It was unforgivable of us. I hope your shoes weren't ruined.'

He wasn't listening but watching her thoughtfully, head on one side. 'You're the very person I need. You can help me with my research.'

She gasped, half with pleasure, half with fright. 'Your research? Oh, but I couldn't. I mean, I don't know anything about playwriting.'

'I'm not asking you to write a play,' he cut her short. 'I've reached a sticky bit. I need to know if something will work or not.' Still he studied her, like a photographer sizing up his subject. 'Yes, you'll do fine.'

He relieved her of the teapot and placed it somewhere behind the door then stepped over the threshold and marched off across the courtyard as if expecting her to follow. A glance over his shoulder showed him she was still standing where he had left her. 'Come on, then,' he called impatiently. 'All right, if you don't want to help me . . .'

Suddenly she wanted to. After all it was rather exciting to be asked to help a playwright with his research. She doubted if anyone would be able to resist it.

She trotted after him. 'What do you want me to do?'

He ignored her question and nodded cordially to the boy cleaning the Land-Rover.

Heading for a wrought-iron gate set in a brick wall he said, 'That lad's a good worker. He's on a youth experience scheme.'

'But . . .'

She was talking to herself. Quartermain had passed through the gate and was out of sight.

She paused and ran her fingers over the gate's wrought-iron scrollwork. The design represented a swan and a stork, their long necks crossed. She supposed it was the Quartermain coat-of-arms and made a mental note to enter it roughly in her sketchbook the moment she returned home.

Quartermain came to see what was keeping her.

'I'd like to sketch this some time, if that's all right with you.'

'Yes, yes,' he said offhandedly. 'Now, come along.'

Beyond the gate was a walled rose-garden where a few of the bushes were still flowering with late blooms. They appeared to be old-fashioned varieties and their fragrance subtly permeated the air.

'Stand behind there!' he commanded, indicating a trellis where dead climbing roses clung to the stems.

She meekly obeyed him.

'Now.' he addressed her through the criss-cross of wooden slats. 'Imagine there's a beautiful rose just about here.' He pointed. 'I want you to lean forward to inhale its perfume.

Bring your face right up to the trellis.'

'Like this?'

He gave a grunt. 'Nearer. That's it. Hold it right there.'

Her chin was close against the wood when his face came towards her from the other side and he kissed her startled lips through the little space.

'Oh!' She trembled and backed away quickly. 'Well, really! Of all the nerve!' Help! She sounded like a maiden aunt.

'Great!' he exclaimed. 'It'll work perfectly.'

She came round the trellis to face him, her eyes bewildered, her cheeks aflame. 'Now, look here . . .'

'Thanks.' He eyed her flushed face and smiled to himself. 'All in the cause of art, Miss Stafford.'

'You might have warned me.' She watched him suspiciously. 'I don't believe you had any problem in the first place. You just made it up about the research to take advantage of me.'

'My dear young lady.' He sounded patronising. 'Taking advantage of you never entered my mind.' A devilish grin spread over his face. 'We'd better do it one more time, just to make sure we've got it absolutely right. Whoever heard of one take?'

She glared at him. 'No way!'

He gave a negligent shrug. 'Very well. Thanks for your help. It's very much appreciated.' He suppressed the grin. 'Why

43

don't you come in and have that cuppa now.'

Furious with herself for reacting so strongly to his kiss, she considered refusing.

He must have sensed her reluctance for he said seriously, 'I'd really value your company.'

Well, it would give them an opportunity to get on a better footing, she thought. They were neighbours and ought to make an effort to be civil to each other. Even so she was loath to capitulate too readily. 'I thought you considered tea the world's worst time-waster.'

'Did I say that? Oh, come on!' He marched back to the house, once more taking it for granted she would follow. She did, dragging her steps. He waited for her to catch up then opened the door wide and stood aside for her to enter.

'Make yourself at home.' He ushered her into the study. 'I shan't be a moment. I'll just find my housekeeper.'

She took this chance to take a better look at the room. The desk was still cluttered with books and papers but the sheet in the typewriter was blank.

There was a large diary open on the window-sill and she read 'Kiki Dawn, lunch, the Dorchester' next to the previous Sunday's date. She frowned.

On the filing-cabinet lay a letter acknowledging a hefty donation to a children's charity, the money having been raised by Quartermain organising a 'pantomine-horse derby' involving several well-known actors and actresses. Her eyebrows shot up. For someone who disliked children as much as he did it seemed a strange thing to do.

She had delved unashamedly into the overflowing wastepaper bin when she heard him returning and straightened quickly.

The look he gave her indicated he suspected she had been prying into his personal belongings and she sprang to the defensive.

'The paper in your machine is blank. You were making it up, after all.'

'What a suspicious person you are.' He knelt to rummage among some papers on the floor then stood up and thrust a crumpled sheet under her nose.

She smoothed it out and read: 'Tania and Dominic kiss through the bars of the rose trellis'.

'Oh! I'm sorry.' Why was she always apologising to him? She stared again at the typewriter and asked, 'Why the blank sheet then? No inspiration today?'

'Inspiration?' he snorted. 'What's that? I can't afford to wait for inspiration. I've got a play to finish.'

She grimaced, duly chastened, and looked about for a change of subject. The oak panelling caught her eye and she noticed the swan and stork motif was incorporated in the carving. 'It must be wonderful having your own coat-of-arms. What does it denote?'

'Fidelity and fertility.' His mouth quirked on the last word.

She said hurriedly, 'It's a lovely old house but don't you find it a bit large for just one person?'

'It was in my family for centuries,' he explained. 'The Quartermains owned most of the area at one time, before they fell on hard times. Death duties, you know. It was always my ambition to buy it back.' He gazed about him. 'Yes, it is a big place and the upkeep is horrendous. The rooms have been neglected over the years but I'm gradually restoring them to their former splendour. I'll show you one day, if you like.'

'Oh, yes please!' She was genuinely delighted. Old buildings fascinated her and were a wonderful source of ideas for her work. 'In a smaller way, I've renovated The Old Smithy.'

There came a knock on the door and Win Pilgrim, still wearing the floral apron and hat, entered with a tray.

'Hello, Felicity. I didn't know it was you.' She gave a conspiratorial smile. 'Fancy you having tea here!'

Quartermain took the tray from the housekeeper's hands and placed it on the desk, sliding notebooks and pencils off the edge as he did so.

'Call me if you want any more,' said Win, underlining the last word before going out.

'Thanks.' He looked up at Felicity. 'Such veiled undercurrents! What was all that about?'

'Just a private joke.'

'At my expense, no doubt.' He eyed the tea-tray. 'Would you like to pour? No sugar for me.'

He settled into a deep leather armchair and watched her busy herself with the teapot. 'But two for you I see.' He took the cup and saucer she proffered. 'How do you keep that trim figure with such a sweet tooth?'

It was a corny compliment and she squirmed inwardly, but he seemed to be trying to be pleasant. 'I do a lot of running about after the children.'

'I'll bet you do!' His brow furrowed. 'What's the set-up? How come you're saddled with them?'

'Saddled?' She took the armchair facing him and stirred her tea. 'You make it sound like a penance. But I love them. My sister died in an influenza epidemic just over a year ago and I'm looking after them for their father.'

He watched her shrewdly. 'And the idea is to marry him one day, I suppose?'

'Oh . . . no . . .' She blushed furiously. 'I'm not . . . he isn't . . .'

'More fool him then.'

She gazed wide-eyed at him, her cup arrested in mid-air. She took a hurried gulp. And choked.

47

Immediately he was out of his chair and patting her on the back. 'Steady on there, Miss Stafford. You seem to be a bunch of nerves. Are those little monsters proving too much for you?'

She recovered her breath and pushed his hand away. 'Not at all!' Deliberately she added, 'They'll definitely be staying. I can assure you of that. Their father depends on me and . . .'

'You want to make a good impression?' he finished sardonically.

He seemed to imply she was only looking after the children in order to ensnare their father into marriage. 'I told you. I love them,' she insisted.

'Yes. So you did.'

She quivered under his steady blue-eyed gaze. 'I'd better be going.' She replaced her cup and saucer on the tray. 'I have work to do.'

'They both stood up and he towered above her. 'And what work is this?' he asked idly.

'Designing and making samples of do-it-yourself furniture kits,' she explained. 'Small items, like flower-pots and coffee-tables, for sale through mail-order outlets.'

'Ah, yes!' He sounded as if he was interested now, not merely making conversation. 'Your aunt said you were a carpenter. She was very proud of you. She was always expounding your virtues. If I hadn't known I'd have taken you for a dress-designer.'

48

She looked surprised. 'Why?'

'Because of your clothes,' he elucidated. He touched the hem of her cape and studied the fringed braiding with its neat whipped-stem stitching. 'This is a very distinctive garment. I haven't seen another like it. Did you design it yourself?'

She felt flattered. 'Yes, I make most of my own clothes.'

'You'd be good with stage costumes, I expect,' he went on pensively. 'And stage scenery. If you are, they'll welcome you with open arms at the local repertory company.'

She thought for a moment. 'Yes, I suppose I could be of some assistance to them. It might be fun and I ought to get involved with local activities.'

He accompanied her into the hall. 'I'll give your name to the stage manager, shall I?'

She nodded. 'Do you write plays for them?'

He gave a short laugh. 'Not for them specifically, but they have been known to perform some of my works.'

'Yes, I suppose they must have. A famous man like you living in their midst.' She had never seen any of his plays, had no idea as to his style and realised she was treading on dangerous ground.

'Famous?' He called her bluff. 'Had you ever heard of me?'

'Why yes, of course . . .'

'And which of my plays do you like best?' he

49

persisted.

'Oh, I don't know . . .'

'Can you name one of them?'

They stepped into the courtyard. 'Not off-hand, no.'

'I thought as much.'

She came clean. 'Well, I haven't time for theatre-going.'

'That's quite all right, Miss Stafford. No need to feel ashamed. Each to his own.'

She felt frustration welling up. Now he would think she was a Philistine, being only concerned with work and domesticity. It shouldn't matter, yet strangely it did. She tried once more. 'Was it always your ambition to be a writer?' It sounded like the stock question on a chat show and she groaned to herself.

'Always.' He accompanied her around the corner of the house. 'The next question concerns whether I write from experience or make it all up. The answer is a bit of both.'

She felt thoroughly deflated. 'I was just interested, that's all.'

'Look me up in *Who's Who*. It will tell you I was born in Hampshire, the only child of a lawyer and schoolteacher, and educated at Charterhouse and Oxford.'

They had reached a solid iron gate which could be used to close off the courtyard. It stood wide open at present and he stopped beside it. 'I must remember to close this and padlock it tonight. Because it's Saturday tomorrow, Miss Stafford. The day the estate dreads.'

Her hazel eyes were puzzled. 'What do you mean?' From the expression of irony on his face, she had a horrible inkling she shouldn't have asked.

'The day those children of yours rampage through like a horde of Vikings.'

'Oh come!' she protested. 'They're not as bad as all that.'

'What you fail to understand, Miss Stafford . . .' He was being pompous again. ' . . . Is that most of the residents here are elderly. They retired here for some peace and quiet. Now it's like living next to a school. It was very selfish of you to force your charges on them, don't you think?'

She refused to be browbeaten. 'Most old people are all the better for some young company.'

'Agreed. But there's young company and young company. Why, only last weekend they were in my orangery shouting and throwing earth about. My head gardener was most upset and came whining to me. To say nothing of the complaints from the irate residents about missing dustbin lids and trampled flower beds. How do you expect me to work with all these problems to sort out? If I get any more trouble I shall have to do something drastic.'

'I'm doing all I can,' she wailed. 'It takes time. You don't understand what they've been

51

through.'

'You have been warned.'

She turned away thoroughly disgruntled, her thoughts written on her face.

'Cheer up, Miss Stafford,' he called pleasantly as if they had merely been passing the time of day. 'Or may I call you Felicity?'

She mentally counted to ten before replying. 'If you must.'

'Such a pretty name and it suits you.'

'Thank you,' she mocked.

'And you may call me Lawson.'

'How kind of you.' If it were up to her she'd have no further contact with him and wouldn't have to call him anything. 'Lawson.' Despite herself, she liked the sound of it on her lips. Then, since they were being so polite, 'Thanks for the tea.'

'My pleasure.'

As she strode briskly through the gateway his deep throaty laugh echoed after her.

All the way home she re-lived their encounter. That kiss! She could still taste it. Her mouth felt tender somehow as if she had been stung by a bee.

Impatient with herself, she dismissed the fanciful notion.

Lawson was undoubtedly a man of charm and breeding, she mused. He had turned the charm on her to begin with, inviting her in for tea and paying her compliments, but he had soon reverted to the snide remarks when he

52

had realised she was immune to his blandishments. It must be irksome for a man who was used to having actresses fall prostrate at his feet, to meet a woman who was not at all impressed by him.

She remembered his supposition that she wanted to marry Crispin and reckoned it was the dramatist in him that made him so perceptive. She couldn't imagine why she had denied it. Over the past few weeks she had thought long and hard and was now convinced she was in love with her brother-in-law.

However, the subject of marriage was a delicate matter. She knew she must proceed carefully and choose the right moment to mention it to Crispin. Sometimes she wondered if he would even contemplate marrying a woman so different from the blonde and glamorous Trish. But time would tell. Perhaps when he came home for Christmas . . .

She smiled wryly as she recalled Lawson's preposterous suggestion that she was using the children to capture Crispin's heart. Nothing could be further from the truth. Loving them, caring for them, kissing life better for them, yes. But using them to make Crispin marry her, never! Talk about putting the cart before the horse. It was the other way round—using him to keep them.

Oh dear, that sounded just as bad. Perhaps Lawson had a point after all. No. Love made all the difference. She loved Crispin.

Indoors, she examined her lips in the kitchen mirror. Nothing. What had she expected—his brand? A laugh bubbled up inside her and she chided herself for behaving like a star-struck schoolgirl!

As she prepared fish and chips for dinner, another glamorous blonde invaded her mind— Kiki Dawn. She frowned. The woman must be on very friendly terms with Lawson to have met him for lunch at the Dorchester. Were they having an affair?

'Ha!' she muttered, viciously digging out the eyes from the potatoes, Kiki Dawn was welcome to the man!

She slept badly that night. Round and round in her thoughts was the fear of losing the children if Crispin decided to marry someone else. She couldn't let it happen. Troy and Bryony were settled now. They all got on so well, they belonged together.

She finally succeeded in dropping off into a restless sleep around four o'clock in the morning but her dreams were beset with images of Lawson kissing her through the trellis. Repeatedly she saw his lips coming towards her and she wriggled to escape him. She awoke tired, with the duvet on the floor.

CHAPTER FOUR

Felicity was intrigued to know what made Lawson tick and directly after the children had left for school she drove to Upton St Jude's public library to borrow a book containing two of his plays.

She put it in the cupboard intending to read it at her leisure but its presence played on her imagination and drew her like a magnet. Surrendering to the tingle of excitement in the pit of her stomach she turfed it from its hiding-place. For the next hour the washing-up remained on the draining-board and the design pens lay idle while she immersed herself in the dramatic written word.

Somehow she hadn't realised the plays would be comedies. *Intimate Charade* was witty and articulate and several times she laughed out loud.

It concerned an eminent QC conducting an affair with a brittle socialite. Funny it undoubtedly was, but running parallel with the humour was an underlying thread of irony pointing to the fickleness of women. Between the laughter Felicity found herself bristling with fury at the way the heroine was portrayed as a gold-digger while the hero came over as a likable but gullible fool. The point of the play seemed to be that the man could not hope to win when up against such a scheming woman and all his troubles stemmed from his association with her.

Felicity threw the book down in disgust, determined not to read another word, but every time she stepped over it she felt the urge to pick it up again. Once more her curiosity got the better of her. She made herself a cup of coffee and curled up in the armchair to read *Goodbye Gianna*.

It was set in Rome and peopled by the members of a decadent high society but here again, woven in amongst the laughter, was the message that women were devils and men suffered accordingly.

She thoughtfully turned the last page. 'Where does he get his ideas from?' she asked Pi, stretched before the fire.

Later, as she dashed round doing the housework she had neglected, Felicity came to the conclusion that Lawson had been hurt very badly. And a woman was at the bottom of it.

*   *   *

As promised, Lawson must have got in touch with the local repertory company because Felicity was contacted by the wardrobe mistress and asked to help with the pantomime costumes. She was pleased to lend a hand and went along to the first rehearsal. They were performing 'Aladdin' which meant oriental designs and gave plenty of scope for her lively imagination.

She took several books on ancient China from the library and sketched basic tunics which she planned to bring to life with exotic trimmings. The company was existing on the proverbial shoestring and fantasy-without-expense was its watchword.

'These are terrific,' said the stage manager when she showed him the sketches. 'You really think they'll look this good when they're made up?'

She grinned. 'Trust me.'

She had wondered if Lawson would show his face at the rehearsals but he didn't, and she was amazed by the little pang of disappointment she experienced.

'Does he ever come here?' she asked the principal boy.

'Occasionally. He does a lot for the company. Apart from financial help, there's a scholarship in his name at the local stage school.'

The actor playing the genie interjected, 'You won't see much of him for a while. These days he seems to be tied up with that new discovery, Kiki Dawn. Helping her learn the ropes, I shouldn't wonder.' He winked. 'He'd better mind or he'll get his head caught in the noose!'

'Wish he'd help me learn the ropes,' murmured one of the chorus girls and the others laughed.

They were a hard-working group of players

and everyone knuckled under to share the various duties. Besides designing and helping sew the costumes, Felicity brought her electric drill along to make some of the scenery.

'I really enjoy it,' she told Win Pilgrim when she met her in Upton St Jude's one and only supermarket. 'I can see what attracts people to the stage.'

'Think you missed your vocation?'

'No. I couldn't act to save my life. But I like being involved behind the scenes.'

They reached the checkout and Felicity said, 'Come and have a cup of coffee.'

'I can't spare the time,' Win replied. 'I must get back to the manor smartish. He's flying to Jersey tomorrow morning and will be wanting all sorts of things done at the last minute. He always does. I know him only too well.'

Felicity grinned. Win always referred to her employer with a pronoun rather than by name.

'What's the occasion?'

'The opening night of his latest play, *No Roses*.' Win grabbed her canvas bag and waited while Felicity paid for her groceries. 'A French actress has been given the lead. She's quite a sensation in Paris, by all accounts.' Win jutted her chin. 'I can't see why that Kiki Dawn has to fly to Jersey too. Just to get her picture in the paper with him, if you ask me. What a blooming cheek! She makes me sick, hanging round him all the time.'

'Does he know a lot of actresses?'

58

'Yes, hundreds.' Win straightened her ever-present hat. 'They swarm over him like wasps over a jampot. They all want him to write a play especially for them and make them famous. They've got some hopes!'

Outside it was raining heavily and Win put up her umbrella. 'I shouldn't talk about him behind his back. I love my job. He's a fascinating man to work for.'

'I suppose he must be,' mused Felicity. 'My aunt told me a bit about him. She didn't know him that well but always made him sound fascinating. It wasn't till I met him that I realised how insufferable he could be.'

Win's shrewd eyes twinkled. 'He's all right deep down. He's quite pleasant with most people. You just seem to have got off on the wrong foot with him. Your aunt thought he was charming. And so do I.'

'How long have you worked for him?'

'Oh, it must be four years now. He's a generous employer. I get time off when I want it and the pay's good. I meet loads of interesting people. What more could anyone ask for?'

Felicity thought she might as well go the whole hog with her questioning. 'Why isn't he married?'

'Spoilt for choice, I shouldn't wonder!' Win's expression grew serious. 'I understand there was someone once, before my time. I don't know the details but apparently it all ended in tears.'

'I thought it had to be something like that.'

Win held the umbrella out. 'Here, come and share this. You'll get soaked.'

'That's all right,' Felicity demurred. 'The rain won't ruin my hair-style. It just makes the curls tighter, that's all.'

'You're lucky.'

'Yes, I hated the curly look when I was a kid but now I don't mind. It has its compensations.'

They splashed through the puddles to the car park where Win made for the Quartermain Land-Rover.

Felicity waved goodbye and dumped her groceries in the boot of her own car.

Driving home she mulled over what Win had told her. To everyone else Lawson was a wonderful guy. So how was it he behaved so cavalierly to her? Perhaps she was being too sensitive where he was concerned, reading too much into his barbed comments instead of letting them wash over her. She didn't usually go to pieces over such trifling matters. She was old enough to have grown immune to innuendos.

Anyway she'd been right about there being a woman in his past. He continued to intrigue her.

The thoughts went round and round in Felicity's head. So Kiki Dawn was going to Jersey with him. It sounded very cosy and looked as if something was going on between the two of them. But where did Vera Valance fit into the scheme of things? There were far too many questions and not enough answers.

The phone was ringing as Felicity unlocked the door of The Old Smithy. She dumped the groceries on the floor and rushed to grab the receiver.

It was Miss Deakin, the headmistress of the school, informing her that Bryony had disappeared from her class. They'd searched the school premises without success. Had she arrived home by any chance?

Felicity trembled. 'I don't think so, but I've only just this minute come in . . .'

'That explains why I couldn't get an answer after trying to ring you for the best part of the afternoon,' the woman said peevishly.

'Oh, I'm sorry . . .'

'I suggest you check your property and if she's not there, alert the police.'

As Felicity replaced the receiver she felt a strange coldness in her spine as if someone had dropped an ice cube down her back.

She quickly checked the house, looking in all the nooks and crannies, and the attic, but the child was nowhere to be found. Outside the bedraggled garden was deserted.

One by one she knocked on the neighbours' doors, but no-one had seen Bryony.

The rain had eased off a bit now. As Felicity stared over the soggy manor lawns, sheer panic overtook her. It would soon be dark and her graphic imagination went into overdrive. Such terrible things happened these days. Kidnapping, muggings, hit-and-run drivers— and worse. The little girl was in her care. If anything had happened to her ... She shuddered. It just did not bear thinking about.

With a certain amount of relief she heard the familiar sound of the golf trolley approaching and she breathed a sigh of relief. Lawson Quartermain might be a pain in the neck, but at least he would know the places to search on the large estate.

She ran along the path and through the kissing-gate as the trolley drew to a halt beside it. In the gathering gloom she could just make out Lawson at the wheel and he seemed to have a burden on his lap. As he clambered down with it in his arms she saw he was carrying the limp form of Bryony.

Both of them were drenched to the skin and not merely from the rain. It looked as if they had been in the stream.

The stream!

'Oh no! Oh God, no!' Felicity cried. 'Lawson! Is she ...?'

The look he directed at her was pure vitriol. 'You wicked irresponsible woman!' he snarled. 'Leaving a young child to play alone by the stream like that! How dare you! You should be horse-whipped!'

Felicity strained to see Bryony's face. 'Is

she . . .' The fearful word stuck in her throat. 'Oh, please tell me she isn't . . .' She grabbed Lawson's arm.

'No, she isn't dead,' he rasped through clenched teeth. 'And no thanks to you.'

He pushed past her and went along the path towards the house. She'd left the door ajar and he crossed the threshold, calling to her over his shoulder, 'Ring the doctor!'

She stared, stupefied.

'Move, woman!'

She picked up the hall phone and scanned the list of emergency numbers. 'What . . . what shall I tell him?'

'That she fell into the stream.' He was already disappearing round the turn of the stairs. 'Tell him I've given her the kiss of life and she's breathing.'

Felicity offered up a silent prayer of thanks at this information.

Shaking uncontrollably, she made the call. Fortunately the doctor was in the surgery at that very moment and he promised to come immediately.

She raced up the stairs to find Lawson in the master bedroom leaning over the child he had placed on the duvet.

Bryony, breathing steadily, opened her eyes. 'Auntie Fliss . . .' She choked and started to cry.

Felicity took the small cold hands and rubbed them gently. 'It's all right, darling. You're safe now.'

It seemed to be a signal for Lawson to lose his temper again. Rising to his full height he said, 'You have no right to be in charge of little children. Leaving them to their own devices while you gad about . . .'

His face was white with rage.

'I didn't leave her,' Felicity protested in amazement. 'She was at school. She . . .'

He wasn't listening. 'Poor little mite! If I hadn't glanced out of my window . . . if I hadn't got there in time, she'd have drowned . . .'

'Yes, and I'm grateful, so very grateful . . .'

'At the earliest opportunity I shall personally make it my business to see that these children are taken away from your so-called care . . .'

Felicity stiffened, her face a mask of indignation. 'You'll what! How dare you make such sweeping condemnations without allowing me to explain the circumstances to you . . .'

'The circumstances are, Miss Stafford . . .' He had reverted to surnames she noted. ' . . . that you are not a fit person . . .'

Her anger boiled over. 'How dare you! Get out of here! Get out at once!'

He stared at her for long moments, breathing noisily.

Bryony gave a little whimper.

Lawson glanced at the child then turned abruptly on his heel and marched from the room, his shoes squelching over the floor. With sudden dismay, Felicity heard him leap down the stairs. The front door was slammed with such force the house rattled to its foundations.

Bryony whispered, 'Did he save my life?'

'Yes, darling.' Felicity bent over the bed again. 'He did.'

'Then why did you shout at him and order him out of the house?'

Felicity shook her head in mystification. 'I don't know. It doesn't make any sense.'

There came a ring on the doorbell.

Felicity jumped up. Thank heavens! He'd come back and she would be able to apologise to him. 'Shan't be a minute!' she told Bryony and rushed down the stairs.

It was Doctor Freedman.

'Hello!' he greeted her brightly. 'Where's the patient?'

It was the first time she'd seen the doctor since she had registered with him soon after the move. In his fifties and prematurely bald, he was dressed quite trendily with a striped shirt visible under his navy blazer, so different from the stuffy old family practitioner of her childhood. He had a pleasing manner and joked with Bryony as he examined her.

'She's going to be all right,' he pronounced at last, putting his stethoscope into his case. 'However I'd like to get her to the hospital, just to be on the safe side. They'll probably want to keep her in overnight. I'll run her there myself, if you like. May I use your phone?'

She indicated the extension on the bedside

table. 'Please help yourself.'

While he waited to be connected he said, 'It was fortunate Mr Quartermain was on the scene or it might have been a different story.'

'Yes,' Felicity murmured, eyes downcast.

'I expected to see him here.'

He began to speak into the receiver and she was spared having to explain.

Roger Freedman made the arrangements then stared into Felicity's face. 'You look as if you're suffering from shock. Would you like a sedative?'

'No, no.' she replied hastily. 'I'm feeling guilty, I expect. Lawson . . . er, Mr Quartermain accused me of neglect. I suppose I was to blame really . . . for not making absolutely sure Bryony knew how dangerous it was to play by the stream by herself.'

'You mean you didn't tell her?' the doctor asked incredulously.

'Yes I did, countless times, but . . .'

'Stop torturing yourself then. You weren't to know she'd skip class. I don't see how anyone's to blame.'

'Quartermain doesn't see it that way.'

'He's probably suffering from shock too. It must have been a traumatic experience for him. Don't you worry, he'll feel differently tomorrow.'

'I wish I could believe you.'

The doctor wrapped Bryony in a blanket and lifted her into his arms.

'I'm coming too.' said Felicity. 'I'll ask one of the neighours to collect Troy from the bus-stop and keep him till I return.' She quickly threw a few clothes and toiletries into an overnight bag then followed the doctor down the stairs. 'I'll just pop over to Mr and Mrs Forester at The Lodge.'

As she opened the door she was surprised to see Win Pilgrim coming along the path.

Win looked anxiously at the bundle the doctor carried past her. 'Is she going to be all right?' she asked Felicity.

'I think so. But what are you doing here?'

'He told me to come over,' Win replied. 'Said you might want to go to the hospital and I'm to do whatever is necessary regarding the little boy. I'm to stay here overnight if need be.'

'How very thoughtful of him.' Felicity's eyes grew moist. What an unpredictable man Lawson Quartermain was, she thought, bawling her out one moment and then behaving like a good neighbour the next. 'After I'd been so . . . horrible to him.'

Win's expression registered surprise. 'You couldn't be horrible to anyone if you tried.'

'Oh, couldn't I!' Felicity ran her fingers through her short curls and shrugged helplessly.

From the driveway came the sound of a car horn blowing.

Felicity hastily gave Win instructions for

collecting Troy from the bus-stop then went out to the doctor's car.

While Bryony was being examined at the hospital Felicity had time to think.

It must have been a terrible shock for Lawson to look out of his window and see Bryony in the stream. How he must have raced the trolley over the lawns to get there in time. The child would have been unconscious by then or he would not have needed to give her the kiss of life. There was no telling how long he had been forced to work on her till she began breathing. No wonder he had been angry. And all she had done was whine and order him out.

The following morning Bryony was pronounced none the worst for her escapade and allowed home. She and Felicity arrived in a taxi and Troy, who had been watching anxiously from the window, rushed out to hug his sister.

'I'll be off then,' said Win, pulling on her coat.

'Thanks for everything.'

'Thank him! It was his idea. He's probably already left for Jersey so you'll have to wait till Tuesday when he gets back.'

'Oh yes. I'd forgotten.' Felicity bit her lip. She felt wretched about the way she had spoken to him and wanted to get her apology over and done with and so clear the air. Now she'd have to stew.

Bryony went in search of the cat and lugged the struggling animal into the kitchen. 'Pi, darling! I never thought I'd see you again. If it hadn't been for Mr Quartermain . . .'

'What happened, Bryn?' Troy wanted to know.

'Well,' said Bryony dramatically, 'We were in the middle of jography when I remembered I'd left Maggie-Ann on the little bridge over the stream.' She stroked the cat's fur the wrong way and was bitten on the hand. 'It started to rain hard and I couldn't leave her there, could I?' she mumbled, sucking her wound, 'When I left her in the rain before she wouldn't speak to me for a week.'

'But how did you get away from the school without any of the teachers seeing you?' asked Felicity.

'I asked Mrs Saunders if I could go home to rescue Maggie-Ann and she said no, Miss Deakin wouldn't like it. I told her it was 'portant but she wouldn't listen. So I asked to be excused and crept through the hole in the hedge . . .'

'That was very naughty.'

'Yes, I'm sorry.' Tears overspilled the child's eyes, splashing on to the cat. 'I didn't mean to be bad.'

'But how did you manage to fall in the stream?' demanded Troy.

'I was running over the bridge with Maggie-Ann and she fell in. I couldn't quite reach her

69

and she was swimming away . . . so I leaned over and—splash!' She looked up at Felicity's distraught face. 'I was bad, wasn't I? I'll never do it again, I promise.'

'I know you won't.' Felicity sighed deeply. 'We owe Mr Quartermain a great deal. When he comes back from Jersey we must go up to the manor and thank him. And I must apologise too.'

'Why?' asked Troy innocently.

'She shouted at him and told him to get out,' Bryony divulged.

'Did you?' Troy's voice filled with awe. 'Cor! Why?'

'I don't think there's any need to go into all that.' Felicity adopted a brisk tone. 'I've got a lot to do today. I must write to your Daddy to tell him what happened.' She shivered. 'I hope he won't blame me too.'

'Will he be cross with me for losing Maggie-Ann?' asked Bryony anxiously. 'Mummy gave her to me the Christmas before she went to heaven. I was going to keep her for ever. And now she's drownded.'

'He won't be cross. He'll only be thankful you didn't drown too.'

*   *   *

Word had spread round the estate about Bryony's unfortunate adventure and several of the neighbours called to enquire how she was.

People were nice and caring when you got to know them, thought Felicity. The parson brought the children picture books of Bible stories, Mrs Barnes baked them a cake, Miss Keen arrived with a Venus fly-trap and the Foresters offered to take them up to London for the day to see the Christmas decorations.

Felicity was pleased to get them out from under her feet for a while. They returned with a present each from Father Christmas.

Felicity invited her neighbours in for a cup of tea all showed them over the house. The elderly couple had been married for more than fifty years and their children and grandchildren were scattered all over Britain. As she intercepted the intimate glances which passed between them she deduced they were still very much in love. It made her wonder if she would ever experience that emotion.

'You've made a good job of the modernisation,' said Mrs Forester. 'Your aunt and uncle liked it as it was but it needed brightening up a bit. It was such a pity Charles died so soon. They seemed made for each other.'

Mr Forester took his wife's hand and gave it a squeeze. 'Like us, m'dear.'

*   *   *

The national newspapers contained reports and photographs of the opening of Lawson's

71

play in Jersey. There he was smiling out from the pages with Kiki Dawn, looking more glamorous than ever in gold lamé, clinging to his arm and gazing wide-eyed into his face.

No Roses had been favourably received by the critics and Felicity was pleased for him. 'Quartermain does it again' was one headline and 'The sex war according to Quartermain' was another. From this she deduced the play contained the usual ingredients of predatory female and gullible male.

On Tuesday evening Felicity was washing-up the dinner things when Lawson called unexpectedly.

He carried a brown-paper parcel in one hand and a bunch of flowers in the other.

Felicity just gaped at him, suddenly tongue-tied.

'Is Bryony about?' he asked.

'I've just put her to bed.' She whipped off her apron and dried her hands on it. 'She won't be asleep yet. You'd better come in.'

CHAPTER FIVE

Lawson placed the flowers on the hall table and followed her up the stairs. Felicity was unnerved by the muffled sound of his footsteps right behind her and almost stumbled in her haste to reach the landing.

She led him into Bryony's room where the night light was burning dimly.

'Are you awake?' Felicity whispered.

'Yes.'

'You've got a visitor.' Felicity turned on the bedside light and the little girl sat up blinking.

'Good evening, Bryony.' Lawson presented the parcel to her. 'That's for you, my dear. I trust you're better after your ducking.'

'Yes, thank you.' She tore at the wrapping. 'It's Maggie-Ann!' she cried ecstatically, hugging the doll.

Felicity looked bemused. 'How ever . . . ?'

'It was caught in the weir-grating downstream,' he explained. 'One of the gardeners found it this morning apparently and Win recognised it.' He crouched down beside the bed and put a hand to Bryony's shining golden head. 'Mrs Pilgrim gave your dolly a spin in the washing-machine. Maggie-Ann seemed to enjoy it.'

'Yes. She likes the washing-machine. She always waves to me as she goes round.'

He managed somehow to keep a straight face. 'I think she looks well, don't you? And none the worse for her swim downstream.'

'She's lovely!' Bryony gazed at him adoringly. 'You rescued both of us.'

'What were you going to say to Mr Quartermain?' Felicity prompted.

Bryony slipped her hand in Lawson's. 'I'm sorry I fell in the water and caused you all the

73

in'venience. Thank you for rescuing me and giving me the kiss of life.'

He smiled. 'You're welcome, my dear, but don't do it again.'

Troy had heard their voices and now appeared, pyjama-clad, in the doorway. His features contained a wistful expression as if he subconsciously resented the attention his sister was getting.

Lawson delved into his pocket and produced a packet of felt-tipped pens marked with an airline logo. 'I had these given to me on the aeroplane. I thought you might like them.'

'Cor!' Troy brightened considerably. 'Thanks!'

Felicity felt a painful lump in her throat. She cleared it noisily.

Lawson looked about him. 'This is a nice room you've got, Bryony. I like your fairy-tale coach. And the horses.'

'Auntie Fliss made them,' said Bryony. 'She made everything. She's clever, isn't she?'

Lawson's eyes met Felicity's. 'Very.'

'Come and see my room,' invited Troy. 'My bed's a pirate ship.'

Lawson cocked an eyebrow at Felicity. 'May I?'

'Please do.'

They went along to admire the decor. Lawson was fascinated by the treasure-island map on the wall and he and the boy discussed it at length.

'Auntie Fliss drew it,' said Troy. 'She's . . .'

'Clever,' finished Lawson, a grin slanting his lips. 'Yes, I know.'

Felicity reminded the children it was time they went to sleep. They reluctantly returned to their beds and she and Lawson retreated down the stairs.

At the bottom she faced him awkwardly, knowing she should say something but aware her mouth had gone dry. As they stood in the little hall, the ticking of the clock and her erratic breathing filled her ears. She heard her heart thumping wildly too. It sounded like a trip-hammer and she wondered if he could hear it.

'I wanted to say . . .' she croaked.

He forestalled her by grabbing up the flowers from the hall table and flourishing them under her nose. 'Please accept these with my apologies.'

'Oh!' She took them wonderingly. The bunch was made up of two or three hellebore blossoms, some winter iris and a few wisps of winter jasmine.

'I can be an insensitive brute sometimes,' he conceded gallantly.

'They're beautiful. You shouldn't have!' She realised she was gushing to cover her embarrassment.

'They're only from the estate. I picked them on my way here.'

'You picked them for me?' She buried her nose in the blooms and inhaled their delicate perfume. 'How kind of you! I feel very privileged . . .' She stopped. No need to go right over the top.

He said, 'I just wanted you to know I'm sorry for the arrogant way I behaved . . .'

'Please don't say another word!' she cried. 'It's I who should be apologising. Shouting at you like that! How melodramatic can you get! The pantomime is obviously having an effect on me.'

'I guess I had it coming,' he muttered grimly. 'Accusing you of neglect! You must forgive me and put it down to the ducking I'd just had.'

'Nonsense! You were entitled to be angry. We'll be forever in your debt. Bryony stayed in hospital overnight, by the way, and they said she was OK . . .'

'I know,' he interrupted. 'I phoned Win from Jersey the next day to make sure.'

She was moved that he had taken the trouble to do that. It showed he really cared. Had she been wrong about him? Where was the child-hater now?

A long silence ensued and he shifted from foot to foot as if he was looking for an opportunity to leave.

'Would you like a drink?' she offered, strangely unwilling to let him go.

He grinned and said, a trifle sheepishly, 'A

cup of tea would go down well.'

She'd been afraid he'd refuse and she beamed. 'Why don't you go and make yourself at home in the sitting-room and I'll bring it in to you.'

She didn't know why but she hummed to herself as she made the tea. Lawson's arrival and generous apology had lifted a weight from her shoulders. She hated arguments, now she felt they could really start again.

When she arrived with the tray she found him sitting on the couch, his long legs stretched out before him, Pi curled up on his lap.

'This cat is a pest,' he grumbled good-humouredly. 'He will keep coming over to the manor. There must be mice in the outbuildings. He won't leave me alone and sleeps on my manuscripts.'

'Would you like me to control him firmly, as well as the children?' she asked, tongue in cheek.

He arched his brows. 'Since when have you controlled the children?'

'Ouch!'

The glimmer in his eyes had told her he was joking and she handed him the cup and saucer. 'There you are. No sugar for you.'

'You remembered.' He spoke softly, giving the statement intimate undertones.

She trembled and looked away, feeling as gauche as a teenager.

77

He laughed, not unkindly, and looked about him. 'I like what you've done in this room. The green and plum is a most attractive combination. And the children's rooms are out of this world. You've worked very hard.'

'Thank you. But it's my job. It's what I know best.'

'And what are you working on at the moment?' he asked politely.

'Designing magazine racks. The company tells me what to make and I work out the design for their approval. Then I send them a working sample and they do the rest. I'm making these particular items in the shape of cartwheels.'

'Show me,' he invited.

She hesitated. 'Oh, you don't want to waste your time . . .'

'Show me.'

Eagerly she fetched one of the finished racks from her workroom. He took it in his strong hands and turned it this way and that, stroking the smooth wood and looking intently at the graining. 'This is excellent. It wouldn't look out of place in Buck House.'

She laughed. 'Don't patronise me, please.'

'No, I mean it.' He passed it back to her. 'With your talent you should be working for yourself, not putting money into the pockets of someone else.'

'Maybe.' She returned the rack to her workroom. When she re-entered the sitting-room, she saw he had leaned his head against the couch and closed his eyes. She noted little stress-lines beside his mouth which made him appear strangely vulnerable. His trip to Jersey would have been exhausting and he must have come here soon after he got back from the airport.

'And how was Jersey?' she enquired softly in case he was asleep.

He jumped and his eyes flew open. 'Forgive me, I was nearly asleep. The trip went very well indeed. The opening night was for charity and there were house-full signs outside. The second night was the important one, career-wise, but it was also fully booked. They're putting on another of my plays in the spring and Kiki Dawn has agreed to play the lead.'

'I see.' She sipped her tea. 'I saw your pictures in the paper. She's a very attractive woman.'

'Yes.' He gazed at her from under half-closed lids, his long lashes casting shadows on his angular cheeks. 'But I've seen as good, if not better.'

'A refill?' she offered quickly.

He glanced at his watch and declined. 'Much as I'd like to. But I made some notes during the flight and I want to collate them.

Felicity accompanied him to the door.

'Thank you for the flowers and ... everything.'

He hooked a finger under her chin and

studied her features. He was close enough for her to detect that distinctive tang of his aftershave.

He said, 'It's been a difficult time for you. You look just about all in.'

'Yes, worrying about . . .' She was going to conclude 'having to apologise to you' but thought better of it.

His eyes remained on her face and she was almost dazzled by their blueness. There seemed to be a certain amount of empathy flowing between them and she hoped he wasn't going to kiss her. It would spoil everything.

His hand dropped to his side. 'Better catch up on your beauty sleep then. Goodnight, Felicity.'

She opened the door and watched him walk away into the darkness, unable to credit the tiny pang of regret at his leaving. Tonight she had witnessed another side of Lawson Quartermain, a kind sympathetic side with a tolerance for kids, which she admired. Was this the same man who had threatened to take her to court if she failed to control them? What a complex character he was turning out to be! Why, she found him almost likable.

Watch it! she told herself as she searched for a vase for the flowers. If she wasn't careful she'd be falling under his spell along with the rest of them.

*   *   *

Crispin, beautifully tanned, his hair bleached white by the Middle-Eastern sun, came home in time for Christmas and Felicity made up the sofa-bed in the sitting-room for him.

After he had unpacked his suitcase he placed a pile of gaily wrapped parcels beneath the tall Christmas tree.

'Not to be opened, or even felt, until Christmas Day,' he told them.

With the children clinging to his waist, he leaned forward to plant an affectionate kiss on Felicity's cheek.

'They're looking well, and so are you,' he smiled. 'I've thought of you often while I've been away, wondering how I had the gall to let you carry out your crazy plan to look after my children. Has it been too terrible, my dear?'

'Tiring,' she admitted. 'But we're winning. Honestly. And I can't imagine life without them now, so stop worrying yourself.'

He took them out for a pre-Christmas lunch at a local hotel and afterwards they walked along the wintry beach, racing each other to the desolate groins and throwing stones into the sea.

That evening when the children were in bed, the two adults enjoyed coffee and liqueurs in front of a roaring log fire.

'How have you really coped?' asked Crispin staring into the leaping flames. 'You can be perfectly honest with me, my dear.'

'I haven't coped too badly actually. They were quite naughty to begin with but they're settling down. And they like school.'

'Bryony's tumble into the stream must have been pretty nerve-racking for you,' he reflected. 'I owe Quartermain a great deal. I shall make a point of thanking him personally at the earliest opportunity. I've brought him a rather rare book I found in a bazaar, about archaeological digs in the Gulf, to show my appreciation. I'll take it over to him in the morning.' He paused. 'Are relations still strained between the two of you?'

'Well, we've called a truce over the accident. In fact he was quite pleasant the last time we met. But I don't know how long it will last.'

'Poor love.' He reached for her hand and played absently with her fingers. 'It's a great comfort to me to know the children are with you. Trish would have approved of our arrangement.' His grey eyes brimmed with sincerity. 'I'm so grateful.'

She smiled tenderly. 'There's no need to keep thanking me, you know. I'm loving it. I must admit I was anxious at first, especially when they upset the neighbours . . .'

'Did they?' he chuckled. 'Don't tell me they upset your dramatist?'

'It doesn't take much to upset him,' she replied darkly and went on to tell him about the mishap with the silver tray and teapot.

'He looked so comical with milk all over his

jeans and shoes, and also very angry,' she finished. 'I didn't know whether to laugh or cry.' She grew introspective. 'I usually get along with people but he and I seem to rub each other up the wrong way. Right from the start he's gone out of his way to needle me. He even tried to dissuade me from moving in. It's almost as if he has it in for me for some reason. Is it me, do you think—or him?'

'Oh him, bound to be!' Crispin covered a yawn with his hand. 'I'm sorry, Felicity, my dear, how very rude of me.'

'Not at all. It's been a long day and you'll be wanting to get to bed.' She pulled the cushions off the sofa-bed for him and unfolded the blankets. 'It's selfish of me to keep you up with my chattering.'

He yawned again and stretched. 'Selfish? You? Don't be ridiculous!' Gripping her busy hands he made her stop what she was doing. 'Leave that. You've done enough for me already. I can make my own bed, you know.'

He opened the door for her and planted a brief kiss on her lips as she passed through. 'Night, Felicity. I'll see you in the morning.'

She stood outside the door for a long time touching her mouth and savouring his kiss. It was marvellous having him here. Why, they were like one big happy family. She wondered if the time had come to talk to him about the future but knew she mustn't rush him. He must be allowed to get over Trish at his own pace.

Yet she had the feeling things were going to work out beautifully for all concerned.

Two days before Christmas, while the Foresters babysat, she and Crispin attended an old-time dance at the community centre in aid of the repertory company.

Felicity wore a simple yellow dress she had made herself and Crispin told her she looked wonderful.

Her glance in turn appraised his silver grey suit which showed off his slender grace. 'And you look positively dashing.'

Felicity was familiar with most of the dances. Her parents were old-time devotees. She and Crispin were soon pleasantly exhausted from stamping out the St Bernard's Waltz, twirling through the Gay Gordons and gliding gracefully around in the Valeta.

Felicity had fully expected Lawson to put in an appearance, considering the theatre was the good cause, but it was not until the interval that he eventually showed up.

He looked magnificent in a dark suit which she guessed would have a Savile Row label. It clung so perfectly to his broad shoulders and long legs. Felicity's mouth fell open at the sight of him. She snapped it shut when she saw his companion.

Kiki Dawn, in slinky ski-pants and low-cut emerald blouse, looked every inch the up-and-coming actress and a barrage of wolf whistles echoed to the steel rafters as she made her theatrical entrance.

Felicity sneaked a glance at Crispin, remembering his penchant for glamorous blondes, and noted he was as captivated as the rest of the men.

'What a beautiful woman!' he exclaimed. 'I expect it's an occupational hazard for successful playwrights to have actresses falling over themselves to be seen with them.' He squeezed Felicity's fingers and added wickedly, 'Lucky old Quartermain!'

Lawson and Kiki spent the interval in the bar. Afterwards they launched themselves vigorously into the dancing, making an attractive couple as they swept elegantly past in the Viennese Waltz.

Felicity came face to face with Lawson in the barn dance where the couples were required to change partners as they progressed in an orderly fashion round the floor.

'Hello there!' His grip was firm as he swung her round. 'Where did you learn to dance so well?'

'Brought up on it,' she shouted above the music.

'Same here,' and he was gone to meet his next partner before she had a chance to dwell on the dubious thrill of being in his arms.

Later he came over to introduce Kiki to them and Crispin was in his element as he drew her aside to tell her all about the oil business.

'It was decent of him to bring me the rare book,' said Lawson, left with no option but to make small-talk with Felicity. 'We had a long chat. I like the guy.'

The band struck up a square tango and Lawson, seeing Crispin was still monopolising Kiki, invited Felicity to dance.

With some trepidation she joined him on the floor. It was a highly dramatic dance and he held her very correctly a foot or so away from him as they waited for the music to start. However the moment the dance began they were thrown together in the general crush.

Felicity was nervous and concentrated on the steps so as not to make a fool of herself in front of him. His chin kept glancing her forehead and she was a mass of nerves by the time they had finished. He dipped her very professionally then led her back to the table.

Kiki, with a daggers-drawn look at Felicity, immediately took his arm and dragged him on to the floor again for the Yearning Saunter.

'I thought you two didn't get on,' observed Crispin slyly.

'I told you, we've called a truce for the moment,' she parried.

In Crispin's close embrace for the last waltz, Felicity sensed Lawson's eyes watching her over Kiki's emerald shoulder. At first she refused to acknowledge him. But the feeling persisted and she turned her head. The blueness of his brooding gaze made her give a little shiver and Crispin asked if she was cold.

'Quite the reverse,' she told him. In fact she was so hot and bothered she was thankful to get outside into the chilly night air.

On Christmas morning, Crispin's parcels were unwrapped to reveal a wonderful assortment of gifts for the children and an Arabian jubbah, meant to be worn as a house-gown, for Felicity. Made from wild silk and featuring a peacock design, it ran like quicksilver through her fingers. 'Oh, my dear, it's beautiful,' she whispered. 'And I'll be able to copy the design.'

'That's what I thought.'

'I think I'm going to cry.'

He looked frankly embarrassed. 'I wanted to get you something special, to show how much I care for you.'

'Oh Crispin!' She threw her arms round his neck, half expecting him to kiss her. When he didn't she gave him a hug and let him go. It was only eighteen months since Trish had died, too soon to make any declarations. She mustn't spoil everything now by rushing her fences.

He donned the embroidered and monogrammed corduroy waistcoat she had made for him. 'Very classy indeed. I'll be the envy of my Club when I get back. You might even get some orders.'

They attended the opening performance of the pantomime on Boxing Day and shouted

87

themselves hoarse with the traditional repartee between audience and actors.

During the interval the people in the bar were commenting on the stunning costumes and at the end of the show the actor playing Abanazar made special reference to Felicity's work. She was applauded and eventually persuaded to rise and take a self-conscious bow.

'Well done!' exclaimed Crispin as they left. 'Aren't we lucky, kids, to have Auntie Fliss in the family?'

She met his admiring eyes over their blond heads and smiled.

In her bedroom that evening Felicity dropped on to the dressing stool and gazed despondently at her reflection in the oval mirror.

Why couldn't she look just a little like Trish? she wondered, pushing her fingers into her tight cluster of curls. Why did it have to be caramel, such a nondescript colour which was neither blonde nor brunette? And her eyes. Why couldn't they be green or brown instead of hazel, that curious hue that was a mixture of both? She looked at her figure. It went in and out in all the right places, she supposed, but it was ordinary. *She* was ordinary.

Her looks were not the problem though. She could bleach her hair, she thought wildly, wear coloured contact lenses, go on a slimming diet, take a course in deportment, learn the social graces, have cosmetic surgery! But nothing would make her a substitute for her sister.

It wasn't in her nature to feel sorry for herself and she laughed out loud. What did it matter what she looked like, for heaven's sake? Troy and Bryony loved her. That was an indisputable fact and the main thing in her favour.

She had undressed and pulled her nightdress over her head when a thought occurred to her that made her squirm. Lawson had accused her of using the children to ensnare their father. From the way her mind had been working just then his remarks seemed dangerously justified.

Drat the man! she thought irritably. Why did he have to keep popping into her mind?

*   *   *

The residents of the estate were invited up to the manor for drinks on the afternoon of New Year's Day.

'Does he always behave like the lord of the manor?' quipped Crispin as they wrapped up warm to venture out into the wintry air.

'Yes, I'm afraid he does. Well, he saved the house from rack and ruin and he's gradually renovating it. I suppose he's entitled to call himself the squire . . .' Felicity was surprised to discover herself defending Lawson but, seeing Crispin's look of amusement, she stopped. 'We

89

needn't go if you don't want to.'

'Do you want to go?' he fielded the decision back to her.

'I ... think we should. I mean, we don't want to look as if we're avoiding him. And the other residents will be there. You should meet them ...' She saw her brother-in-law's eyes crinkle at the edges. 'Have I said something funny?'

'No, my dear, you're right, we should go. And who knows?' he teased her. 'The delectable Miss Kiki Dawn might show up.' Helping her on with her cape, he added, 'We'll have to leave early. I've booked a table at the Swan, remember?'

They trudged over the frosty lawns, hands pocketed, collars turned up, to be greeted at the door by Lawson looking very much the successful playwright in shaggy sweater and designer jeans.

As Felicity handed Win her cape, she was aware of Lawson's eyes on her, and felt unusually pleased with herself.

Having been assured by the housekeeper that the ground floor of the manor house was centrally heated, she had put on a dress of sapphire crêpe with a baggy blouson bodice top held up by the merest of straps. The skirt was tight with a zigzag hem which floated ethereally about her legs. She hoped she looked as good as she felt. Crispin had told her she did, but she discounted his compliments.

He always said what was expected of him.

The manor was decked out in winter greenery and there was a twenty-foot-tall Christmas tree in the hall.

They and the other residents of the estate, along with several noteworthy townspeople, gathered in the games room where a huge log fire roared up the stone chimney. A wooden cover was on the snooker tale on which an inviting spread of snacks and canapés had been set out. Extra staff had been engaged and waiters weaved among them with trays of drinks.

Troy immediately tried to make an impression on a punchball in the corner of the room, while Bryony clambered on to Mrs Forester's lap to show her a new doll and its various underclothes.

'At least we've made some friends on the estate,' murmured Felicity, nibbling at a cocktail sausage. 'At first I thought we never would. What with all the complaints we received about the children's behaviour. It just shows that people aren't so intolerant after all when you get to know them. And the kids are better behaved these days.'

Crispin took two glasses of white wine from a passing tray and handed one to her. 'The Foresters seem nice people. And they obviously like children.'

'Hm, yes.' Felicity glanced across at the elderly couple, admiring their calm easy relationship.

'They've been married for over fifty years,' she told Crispin. 'They seem to have a built-in radar system whereby each knows instinctively what the other is thinking.' It really was uncanny sometimes, she thought to herself. It must be magnificent to share a love like that. What would it be like to be adored as Mrs Forester was adored?

'What are the other residents like?' Crispin interrupted her train of thoughts.

'Miss Keen is a bit of tartar,' said Felicity, pointing out the tall delicately boned woman with grey hair cut in a Cleopatra fringe. 'She was a headmistress in her heyday and is used to being obeyed. But she's unbending a little. She gave me some holly from her garden the other week.'

Felicity glanced to where the parson was in deep conversation with crotchety old Mrs Barnes. 'Those two will take a bit longer coming round. The parson is a Deep Thinker and seems to live on another planet, but he's always civil to me. They say he's writing a book about the parish church. And old Mrs Barnes might look like your idea of a lovable grandmother, but she enjoys a good grumble.'

Crispin wasn't listening. Kiki Dawn, dressed from head to toe in figure-hugging black leather, her long hair loosely tied in a white scarf, had made one of her sensational entrances.

CHAPTER SIX

All male eyes, including Crispin's, were on the young actress.

Kiki had eyes only for Lawson.

He poured her a drink and she talked quietly with him, to the exclusion of everyone else.

Crispin took Felicity's elbow. 'Much as I'd like to stay. I think we'd better get going. I booked the table for six o'clock.'

Troy piped up. 'Can't we stay for another five minutes?' He was trying his luck on an old-fashioned fruit-machine which took pre-decimalised pennies, thoughtfully provided.

'Just five minutes then,' said Crispin.

Presently, they were doing the rounds saying their goodbyes to Lawson and the neighbours when Vera Valance arrived.

She wore a scarlet suit and her thick black hair was a rich haze about her shoulders. As she breezed in Felicity caught a whiff of expensive perfume.

Vera's eyes raked the company and came to rest on Kiki. She forced a bright smile. 'I didn't know you'd be here, darling.'

'Why ever not?'

Crispin eyed the two actresses in turn and whispered in Felicity's ear, 'Goldilocks meets the Queen of Hearts.'

She dug him hard in the ribs. 'Shush! They'll

hear.'

The two women kissed cheeks.

'Let battle commence,' murmured Crispin.

Vera said, 'I thought you were appearing in a play in Glasgow, darling.'

'It was postponed.' Kiki perched herself on the arm of a chair and swung her endless legs. 'So, when Lawson begged me to grace his little party, how could I refuse?'

'How indeed!'

Lawson watched them, his expression unreadable.

Mrs Forester asked cordially, 'When are we going to see you at the local theatre again, Miss Valance?'

Vera placed her empty glass on a tray and took a full one. 'I haven't much time these days to appear in rep.' She looked quickly at Lawson. 'I might be appearing in a Manchester production of *Hamlet* in the New Year.'

'One up to the Queen of Hearts,' was Crispin's low comment.

'Why, that's wonderful news,' said the old lady. 'Have you a good part?'

Vera hesitated. 'The cast list hasn't been finalised yet.'

'Well, I think you should,' said Mrs Forester loyally. 'I remember seeing you in Shakespeare many years ago and I thought how marvellous you were.'

Kiki gave a brittle laugh and Vera blushed beneath her flawless make-up.

'Oh dear,' breathed Crispin. 'Whose side is the old girl on?'

Quite oblivious to the tension in the room, Mrs Forester went on blithely, 'The newcomers to the business don't seem to have the same flair as the old-timers.'

'Game, set and match to Goldilocks,' said Crispin. 'I'll get the kids.'

Felicity stilted a laugh. 'And I'll get our coats.'

She crossed the hall to a small cloakroom where Win had put the cape and the three duffed coats.

A glance in the mirror assured her she still looked good. She was tucking a rogue curl behind one ear when she heard a sound behind her and saw, in the reflection, Lawson enter the room. She swung round to face him.

He closed the door and leaned nonchalantly against it, a little smile playing about his lips.

'You look sensational, Felicity.'

She had never considered herself capable of looking sensational, no matter what Crispin or anyone else insisted, but now that Lawson had said so, she felt it must be true. 'Thank you.'

For a measureless moment they gazed at each other. She wanted to look away but was incapable of movement. It was like being under the influence of a mesmerist.

He blinked. 'Must you go? It's early yet.'

'I'm afraid so.' She reached for her cape. 'It's been very nice, but Crispin's booked a table for dinner.'

He took the garment from her. As he draped it around her shoulders his fingers glanced her neck. She shivered.

He said, 'I came for my New Year kiss.'

She turned to gape at him. 'Wh . . . what?'

'You heard me!' He pouted playfully. 'Please?'

How could she refuse? She offered her cheek.

He ignored it. Instead he eased her into his arms and his lips, warm and passionate, covered hers. She was too surprised to resist him and was plunged into a deep well of desire. It set her heart galloping and, clinging to him, she yielded to her natural instinct to return his kiss.

There was a sensual glow in his eyes as he slowly released her and, for a moment, he appeared as bewitched as she. Then his eyes became hooded and he said, 'Well, well! Who'd have thought it?'

'Thought what?'

'That you contained such heated emotions beneath that calm don't-touch-me exterior.'

She wished she hadn't reacted so positively to his kiss and asked shakily, 'Is that from one of your plays?'

He slid his fingers carelessly through his dark haze of coppery hair. 'It was just a New Year kiss.'

She detected undertones of self-mockery in

96

his voice and didn't know what to make of him.

'You'd be wise not to set any great store on it.'

'Don't worry,' she declared. 'I won't.'

He smiled, in command of his feelings now and enjoying her discomfort. 'Well, well!'

'Will you please stop saying that!' she snapped. She recalled his twisted view of women. How sweet it would be to cut him down to size. 'It must be very frustrating for you to meet a woman who doesn't think you're God's gift, but I'm afraid you're going to have to live with it.'

'Is that so?'

She headed for the door but he barred her way.

'Please let me pass. Crispin will be waiting.'

'Ah, we mustn't keep Crispin waiting.' He stood aside and asked bluntly, 'Are you going to marry him?'

'Yes, I am!' She wrenched open the door. 'If it's any of your business.'

'Felicity!' The word cracked out like a gunshot.

She took a deep breath and turned. 'What is it now?'

He had picked up the three duffel coats. 'Don't forget these.'

She snatched them away from him and marched outside, knowing he was following.

Crispin's gaze took in her grim expression. Helping the children into their coats, he asked,

97

'What's up, love?'

'Nothing at all.' She linked her arm deliberately in his. 'Come on, dear, let's get out of here.'

She had meant to sweep out without a further glance in Lawson's direction but couldn't help herself. He was watching her with a deep unfathomable expression on his face. A curious little quiver ran through her and she almost bolted in her eagerness to escape his presence.

As the taxi whisked them across town to their destination, her nerves throbbed with the recollection of Lawson's kiss. She had been kissed before, but never with quite so much audacity and certainly never so much passion. Why had she made such a fuss? A New Year kiss couldn't be considered a reason for hysterics. But was it a New Year kiss? She thought not. So what was he playing at?

The Swan was an old coaching inn and she had been looking forward to sampling its fabled cuisine, but afterwards could not remember anything she had eaten. It was Lawson's fault. Why did he have to spoil things all the time?

Later, after she and Crispin had tucked the children up in bed and he had read them each a story, she went off to change into the house-gown he had given her.

When she arrived downstairs he was standing in front of the sitting-room fire examining the Christmas cards on the mantelpiece. Among them were those from her far-flung family, her parents in Spain, two brothers in Canada and New York, and her sister in Scotland.

The family always phoned each other on New Year's Day. That morning she had had a long conversation with her mother who had wanted to know what she was doing about finding herself a husband.

Felicity had tried to sound vague, but Mrs Stafford detected the excitement in her voice.

'Who is he? Do we know him? It's not that playwright fellow you told us about in your letters, is it?'

Felicity was glad her mother could not see her face. 'Don't be silly, dear, he's the last person.'

'Pity, he sounded charming.'

Crispin turned and caught his breath as she entered. 'You look lovely, Felicity.'

'Thank you.' She slipped her arm through his. 'Crispin, you are pleased with the way I'm looking after the children?'

He squeezed her arm. 'Lord yes! Why do you ask?'

'Well, we all seem to get on so well.' She summoned up her courage and ploughed on, picking her words carefully, not wishing to seem insensitive but desperate to have the future settled. Besides being the children's father he now appeared as a protective wall

99

standing between her and Lawson. 'It's wonderful us all being together . . .'

'My dear!' He kissed the top of her head.

Impulsively she threw her arms round his neck and hugged him. 'It's wonderful us all being together,' she repeated. 'Not just at Christmas time . . .'

He misunderstood her. 'Have I been a bit offhanded, Felicity? Is that why you're worried that I don't appreciate you? I'm sorry, it's just that, well, at this time of year I tend to think about Trish . . .'

Of course he did! He was such a caring person he was bound to think of all the good times they had shared. She moved away from him, not listening to what he was saying, thankful she hadn't revealed what was in her heart and ruined her hopes and dreams.

' . . . And New Year was when I proposed,' he finished.

'I understand,' she whispered and, taking a leaf out of Lawson's excuse book, added, 'By the way, that was my New Year hug. I wish you all that you wish yourself.'

'You're a sweet girl, Felicity.'

A few days later Crispin returned to the Gulf and things settled back into the routine. Then in the middle of January, Felicity was called to London for a meeting at the furniture-makers for whom she worked.

She was used to occasional meetings which were usually held to discuss new lines. Today was different however. The managing director announced sadly there had been a takeover and changes were inevitable. The home-workers would no longer have a free rein for their ideas.

Felicity was profoundly disappointed and could see the other home-workers were similarly affected. They were given a week to think about it but she made up her mind there and then. She had enjoyed the work and the freedom of setting her own pace and didn't relish being subjected to stringent controls. If the job brought no pleasure she might as well give it up.

Later on the train home she hoped she hadn't been too hasty. It certainly looked as if the time to branch out on her own had finally arrived and she felt a sudden surge of excitement.

The moment she arrived home she crossed to The Lodge to collect the children from the Foresters but the house seemed to be deserted. Hearing voices from the rear of the property she went round to investigate. The elderly couple were staring anxiously at a brick building which stood on Lawson's land and was used for storing the estate's gardening machinery and various supplies. Of the children there was no sign.

'What's going on?'

'Oh, Felicity!' said Mrs Forester, 'The children ran into the store about fifteen minutes ago and something's fallen across the door and trapped them . . .'

The children called out and Felicity rapped on the invincible-looking cast-iron door. 'Don't panic! I'll soon have you out.' How, she did not know.

Mr Forester said. 'I thought it might be dangerous, what with the cans of petrol and canisters of weedkiller and all that machinery, so I've phoned Mr Quartermain. He'll be here any moment.'

As he spoke the golf trolley rolled across the manor lawns towards them. Lawson looked extremely annoyed.

Felicity hadn't seen him since the afternoon of that audacious New Year kiss and, as he alighted, it immediately sprang to the forefront of her mind.

'Where have you been?' he demanded irritably.

She was tired and didn't want another slanging match with him. 'It's none of your business.'

'Well, while you were off gallivanting,' he grated out, 'those children of yours have got themselves into trouble again.'

'You sound as if I went out and left them unattended,' she said indignantly. 'Mrs Forester was looking after them . . .'

'She can't be expected to control two lively children.' His expression was granite-hard. 'You opted to look after them, so you shouldn't unload your responsibilities on to other people.'

'How did they get in the store in the first place?' Felicity demanded. 'Isn't it kept locked?'

'It is,' he replied grimly. 'One of the gardeners must have forgotten . . .'

'I see.' She treated him to a look of disdain. 'You are responsible for ensuring your employees keep this door locked, so it's your fault.'

He glared at her. 'If you want to put it like that.'

Troy called, 'Please get us out, Auntie Fliss. Bryony's scared and I've cut my hand. And Pi doesn't like it in here.'

'Don't worry!' She met Lawson's gaze challengingly. 'Mr Quartermain will get you out.'

Bryony began to cry. 'Are you going to smack us?'

'No, darling . . .'

'Is Mr Quartermain angry?' asked Troy.

She eyed Lawson wryly. 'No, he isn't angry.'

He pushed her aside impatiently. 'Enough of this nonsense!' He shouted to Troy. 'I'm not going to punish you. Now, tell me, what's fallen across the door?'

'It's a big black pipe.'

'Sounds like the old stovepipe,' muttered Lawson. Raising his voice he said, 'Keep calm, I'll have you out of there in a jiffy.'

103

He drove back to the manor and returned with an extending ladder strapped to the side of the trolley.

Tight-lipped, he placed the ladder against the store and climbed to the skylight, covered with chicken wire, on the sloping roof. There he took a pair of clippers from his pocket and cut through the wire.

'Troy!' he shouted. 'I'm going to break the window. You two take cover behind the tractor.'

'And Pi?' called Bryony.

'And Pi,' said Lawson wearily. 'Give a shout when you're ready.'

A few moments later came the cry, 'Ready!'

Lawson hit the glass with the clippers then tapped all round the edge until every fragment was removed. This done he lowered himself into the aperture.

Felicity heard a scraping sound as he lifted the pipe away from the door. A moment later it opened and Pi flew out, spitting angrily, followed by the frightened children.

As they rushed to the safety of her side, Felicity silently admitted a grudging admiration for Lawson which she couldn't, wouldn't put into words.

He was examining Troy's palm. 'How did you cut yourself?'

'I tried those big scissors. They're really sharp.'

'He means the garden shears, I imagine,'

said Lawson. 'A trip to the doctor's for an anti-tetanus jab seems to be on the cards.'

Felicity passed a shaky hand across her brow.

'I'll take him if you like,' offered Lawson.

'But I couldn't put you to all that trouble,' she murmured half-heartedly.

'Aw, let him take me,' pleaded Troy. 'I want to ride in the Lotus Turbo.'

'Guess that settles it,' said Lawson, already striding towards the trolley with Troy running in his wake. Over his shoulder he shouted, 'I'll send someone down straight away to secure the store door—and mend the window.'

'That's twice Lawson's rescued me,' said Bryony.

'Yes,' muttered Felicity sarcastically, 'He's turning out to be a regular knight in shining armour.'

Mrs Forester was upset at not having looked after the children better.

'Don't worry,' said Felicity. 'It wasn't your fault. Lawson was right, it is my duty to look after them.'

Bryony was in bed when Troy and Lawson returned. Felicity met them on the doorstep.

'The Lotus is brilliant!' said the boy. 'It goes from nought to sixty in six and a half seconds. It can do a hundred and forty miles an hour flat out.'

'I hope it didn't.'

'No, it didn't, worse luck.' He showed her a

plaster on his arm. 'The jab didn't hurt a bit. Dr Freedman said I'm brave.'

She looked at his dirty smiling face. 'You'd better go up and have your bath, then I'll bring you some supper.'

He bounded up the stairs.

Her eyes met Lawson's guiltily. 'Once more I have to apologise. I really am sorry.' She forced a smile. 'I hope you weren't in the middle of a difficult scene.'

'I was, as a matter of fact.' His expression was tense. 'You shouldn't take advantage of Mrs Forester's good nature. Looking after two children is a full-time occupation . . .'

'Well, it will please you to know I shall be looking after them full time in future,' she parried. 'Because I've just lost my job.'

She had expected some sort of comment, a little sympathy perhaps, but should have known better.

He continued from where she had cut him off. ' . . . I don't know why you took on those two. You obviously find them more difficult to manage than you thought. Why don't you give up before they get too attached to you?'

She thought, how typical of him! She was all set to apologise and try to be friends but he wanted to prolong the antagonism. 'They're already attached to me. And I to them. They're no trouble at all. You're to blame for that business this afternoon. You admitted it. You can't leave a door open invitingly and not

106

expect children to investigate. I'm not giving them up. I love them . . .'

'Do you? Isn't it just a ploy to hook their father?'

There! He'd said it again!

'No, it isn't and that's a very unkind thing to say.' With that she firmly closed the door.

She regretted her action immediately. He'd got the children safely out of the store and been good enough to run Troy to the doctor's and she'd shut the door in his face. Why couldn't they be civil to one another? Why was it always like this?

She went into the kitchen to get Troy's supper and had started on scrambled eggs, when she heard a rattling noise. Out of the corner of her eye she saw the window, which she had left on the catch, being opened wide.

She jumped as Lawson stuck his head inside. 'Did you say you'd lost your job?' He spoke calmly now, his anger completely burned out.

She nodded and frantically stirred the mixture in the saucepan.

'If you want a job, I might be able to help.'

She stared at him, bemused. 'I thought you said looking after children was a full-time job.'

'It is. I'm offering you a part-time job.'

'You'd better come in.' She opened the back door.

'The manor house needs more work done on it.' He rescued the toast from under the grill. 'You're a designer. You work with wood. I thought you might like to have a go, on the skirtings and built-in cupboards. The furnishings too, if you feel up to it. I'd pay you, of course.'

The breath caught achingly in her throat. It sounded a marvellous proposition, restoring the manor's ancient fixtures and furnishings to their former glory. It was the kind of job she had often dreamed about and which might come her way but once in a lifetime.

She couldn't accept. Working in the same house as Lawson would be sheer madness.

'Thank you, but no. We'd murder each other.'

'Perhaps you're right.' His lips twisted wryly. 'It was just an idea.' He perched on the kitchen stool. 'How come you lost your job?'

He was the last man she had envisaged opening her heart to but suddenly it all poured out. 'Do you think I should branch out on my own? Or try for similar employment?'

'Go it alone!' he said firmly. 'Home-workers never get a fair deal. You shouldn't have an employer. With your talents, you should be working for yourself.' He drummed his fingers on the table. 'That bedroom furniture you made for the children. I've never seen anything like it. Your use of colour is striking. Then there was your scenery for the pantomime. Yes, I did see it. I only wish some of the scenery for my plays were half as good.'

For a moment she was overwhelmed by his praise. 'Thank you.' She put eggs, toast and a glass of milk on a tray. 'I'll just take this up. Make yourself a cuppa.'

When she returned he was pouring tea into two mugs. 'Yes, go it alone,' he reiterated, sugaring hers and stirring it. 'And in a short time you'll have homeworkers of your own.'

'Hey!' A combination of excitement and apprehension travelled through her. 'I don't know if I dare.'

He snorted derisively. 'I think you dare, Miss Stafford. For someone who would take on a couple of someone else's children, I wouldn't think starting up your own business would hold any terrors. I suggest you work on a new kid's bedroom theme and see how it goes.'

'Yes, that's what I thought . . .'

He snapped his fingers. 'I've got another idea. You'll need somewhere to display your wares. I have a friend with a small shop in Upton St Jude. I'm sure Rosalinda would be delighted to lend you her window.'

'Rosalinda?' she echoed scathingly. 'Not another of your adoring actresses?'

His eyes glittered like two hard pebbles. 'That remark is beneath contempt.'

Her cheeks burned. 'Sorry. I didn't mean . . .'

His tone changed subtly. 'Did I detect a hint of jealousy there?'

109

'Jealousy!' She took a gulp of the scalding tea and spluttered. 'Because of you? Really! Where do you get your quaint ideas from?' She stopped. It sounded like protesting too much.

He grinned smugly as if coming to the same conclusion.

They were standing close together and now that the conversation had taken a personal turn, she was reminded once more of his New Year kiss. She stared at his mouth and swallowed hard. With his towering height and broad shoulders, he seemed to fill the kitchen and she felt suffocated by his masculinity. She gave a little shiver and retreated to the far side of the table.

His gaze followed her steadily, the piercing blue eyes missing nothing. It was almost as if he were reading her mind. Self-consciously, she began tidying the bread and the butter away.

He said, 'Yes, Rosalinda will help. I'll speak to her. Though why I should, when all I get from you is aggravation . . .'

'Yes, why are you being so obliging?'

'A good question. I don't know. I must want my head examined. Well, shall I speak to Rosalinda?'

'Yes, please.'

She placed their empty mugs in the sink. When she turned back to him she caught him looking at her with what could only be described as a wistful expression on his face.

It was gone in a flash. 'I'll be off then. I've got a scene to finish. I only hope I can recapture my train of thought before I was interrupted.'

Later, as she washed up the mugs she contemplated the enigma that was Lawson Quartermain—with her one moment, against her the next—and couldn't help wondering what had happened in his past to make him so cynical about women.

*   *   *

Troy joined the local table tennis club and Bryony started ballet lessons. Both activities took place on Saturday afternoons and gave Felicity more time for working out her new designs.

Nothing had come of Lawson's offer to speak to his friend about the use of the shop window and she guessed it was just a ploy to make her feel grateful. She admitted she was being a little unfair because Win had told her he was attending a first night in New York, but she reckoned she couldn't count on his help.

She started on a jungle theme, her most ambitious project to date. The bed represented a tree-house, the wardrobe and dressing-table an elephant and a lion. She sewed mosquito nets from muslin, made creepers from ropes and carved spears and cooking-pots. The lampshade was a full jungle moon. She designed her own *Tarzan and the Apes* wallpaper and arranged for it to be made up by a local manufacturer who promised early delivery.

For four weeks she sawed, planed, painted and sewed, bringing her ideas to life, by which time the wallpaper was to hand. All that remained was to dye the material for the duvet cover and curtains in a mixture of leafy greens. When she had finished she was exhausted, mentally and physically, but also very excited.

One evening the phone rang and a husky voice announced it was Rosalinda. 'Lawson got in touch with me before he went to the States. Sorry I haven't contacted you sooner but I've been in hospital with bronchitis.'

Felicity expressed her sympathy and said she would bring the furniture to the shop the following day.

As she helped the driver load the heavy pieces into the hired van, she thought how she had misjudged Lawson in this instance.

Rosalinda was an ex-actress, in her eighties at least, with skin like parchment, high-piled hair the colour of antique silver and a figure comparable to that of young woman. In a tangerine jumpsuit, her wrists jangling with bracelets, she seemed a bit over the top for Upton St Jude.

She traded in paste jewellery and had emptied her window ready for Felicity's goods. However the shop was tucked away in a little street behind the supermarket and Felicity wondered if her items would ever be noticed.

Rosalinda viewed the unloading with interest. 'Why, this stuff is heavenly! Any child will love this.'

'You don't think I've priced it too high?'

Rosalinda squinted at the price-tag. 'Are you joking?'

They arranged the items in the window and agreed that Rosalinda would take ten per cent of all orders she received. Each jungle theme would be slightly different to preserve its exclusiveness.

Felicity went home and had hardly got in the door when Rosalinda phoned to say she had two orders already and how soon could she deliver?

CHAPTER SEVEN

Felicity was thrilled by the speed with which her bedroom design had been snapped up. But now she was faced with a problem she hadn't anticipated—fulfilling the orders within a reasonable time. The original sample had taken four weeks and she felt that was too long.

The only way she was going to get over this difficulty was by employing a carpenter to help her.

She got straight on to the Jobcentre and was given the name of a local craftsman.

Danny, a wiry fifty-year-old, had given up regular employment a year earlier to look after his sick wife, Hilda, and welcomed the chance to work from home. Felicity examined a bookcase he had made for himself and hired him on the spot. To her delight she discovered his wife, although bedridden, was a dab hand at needlework and it was agreed she would help with the soft furnishings.

Then it was back home to get out her sketch books and work feverishly on the exclusive differences of the jungle design, one set to be completed by herself, the other by Danny and Hilda. In a couple of weeks both bedrooms were finished and she had come up with a new theme built round a gipsy caravan bed. As in the previous case the orders rolled in within twenty-four hours.

'I might as well give up the jewellery,' said Rosalinda happily, 'I'm making far more out of your bedrooms than I ever did with the other stuff. When can I expect the next masterpiece? People are wanting to know. Your bedrooms are becoming a talking point, my dear. Everybody who's anybody wants one.'

'I've made four more rough sketches of themes I want to do,' said Felicity keenly. 'A spaceship, eskimos, a circus and cowboys. I wondered if we could advertise my services in the local press, inviting people for a consultation to work out between us just what they would like. You know, custom-built for the child in question.'

'What a marvellous idea!' enthused Rosalinda. 'I'll get on to the paper straight away.'

'The thing is,' mused Felicity, 'I really want a wallpaper manufacturer to come in with me. It's costly having it made to my design. Any suggestions?'

'That's no problem,' said Rosalinda. 'My kid brother, young Jolyon, has a finger in lots of local pies. Wallpaper should be right up his alley.'

'Bless you!' grinned Felicity.

She was introduced to 'young' Jolyon the following day. A sprightly septuagenarian, sporting a grey moustache and a bright yellow cravat, he was excited about joining the venture.

By the time Crispin arrived home for the Easter break Felicity was making a name for herself in Upton St Jude and even further afield. He was delighted for her.

'It is rather exciting,' she agreed. They were sitting on the patio enjoying the spring sunshine while the children played tag among the currant bushes.

'And what does Lawson Quartermain make of it all?' asked Crispin.

'I haven't seen much of him lately.' She shielded her eyes to watch a blackbird singing

115

its heart out in the cherry tree. 'Apparently he took a break in Miami after New York. Now he's busy working on his next play, Win says. Actually he got me started, indirectly. At least he found Rosalinda for me and it all went on from there.'

Crispin gazed into her shining hazel eyes. 'I hope you're not setting too much store on Lawson's interest. I don't want to see you hurt, my dear. You're vulnerable, you know, more than you think. He could so easily play fast and loose with your emotions. There are plenty of his sort in the Gulf. Adventurers, we call them.'

Two pink spots appeared on her cheeks. 'I'm not in the least interested in Lawson Quartermain. Believe me, the less I see of him the better.' Then as an afterthought, 'In any case I don't think he's quite as black as you paint him.'

Crispin smiled affectionately. 'You are a sweet little innocent, Felicity. I find it very appealing.'

'Do you?' She gazed at him, her eyes exceptionally wide, and held her breath, wondering if this was the chance she had been waiting for.

'Crispin . . .'

But at that moment there echoed an exaggerated scream from the garden. Crispin got anxiously to his feet and ducked under the cherry tree, calling, 'Troy! What are you two up to?'

'They're OK,' said Felicity, going after him. 'They're playing. They scream differently when they're hurt.'

'You've come to know them rather well, my dear.'

'Yes. I really can't imagine life without them now. We're so happy together. And they're both in excellent health. They've put on weight and Bryony hasn't had an accident for months. This life agrees with them.'

'I know. It's all your doing.'

He fell silent, staring into space, and she realised she was getting nowhere. On a sudden impulse she stood on tiptoe and lightly kissed his mouth. She felt a tiny response almost like a reflex action and drew back.

He grinned easily. 'What was that in aid of?'

'Oh, I don't know. Because you're nice I suppose.'

'As I said, you're a sweet girl, Felicity.'

The children came running up and Felicity went indoors to see about the evening meal, determined that before this weekend was through she would have settled matters with Crispin.

Her opportunity came the next morning after the Easter Day service at St Jude's, the fourteenth-century church where the children attended Sunday School. Directly after the service Mr and Mrs Forester invited Troy and Bryony back to their home to collect some

Easter eggs and Felicity and Crispin were left to return alone.

Spring had come early this year and the hedgerows burgeoned with young leaves, while the air was filled with the unmistakable scent of new growth.

Crispin caught Felicity's hand and tucked it under his arm. 'This is what I miss most,' he confided, 'The normalness of family life. You can't know what it's like living in a hot arid country so different from England. Most of us sit and dream of winter snow and spring rain.' He went on wistfully, 'Perhaps I should try to transfer to a job in England after all. At least I would see the children more often. And you.'

It was now or never, she decided. 'Have you thought about marrying again?'

He caught his breath sharply. 'Why, no.'

'You should, you know.' Her voice shook with emotion. 'You owe it to the children. And to yourself. You're a young man still.'

He shook his head sadly. 'You're right, I know. But somehow, I can't bring myself even to consider it. I feel as if it would be a betrayal of Trish.'

'I think she'd understand,' she said gently. 'She'd want the children to have a mother, I'm sure.'

'Maybe.' He was silent for a long time. 'The trouble is I was so happy the first time it might be unwise to tempt fate a second time. And if I made the wrong choice...' He shivered.

118

'Frankly, it scares me.'

His words warned her not to press him further. 'Why don't you think about it?'

'Yes, I'll certainly do that.'

And with that she had to be content. At least it was a step in the right direction, she consoled herself.

She drove him to the station the following morning and he said goodbye on the platform, first swinging Bryony up in his arms then shaking hands solemnly with Troy, who had decided he didn't like all that kissing stuff.

Lastly Crispin turned to Felicity and pulled her into his embrace. He gave her a mighty hug and kissed her cheek, then jumped aboard the train. She waved as it moved out, remembering their conversation the day before and hoping her dream of them being together was perhaps a little nearer.

Her thoughts had a calming effect on her. There! It hadn't been so difficult after all. Now she had broached the subject things could only move forward. It would take time, that was all, and she was prepared to wait. He would be able to think about what she had said during the long evenings away. Why, when he came home again in the summer he might very well propose.

She did love him, she thought fiercely. She loved his quiet manner and easy-going nature. She loved his fair hair and freckles. She loved his sparkling blue eyes. She loved his company;

she loved . . .

Just a minute, did she say *blue* eyes? She meant grey eyes, of course she did. Nice gentle grey eyes.

She chewed her lower lip thoughtfully. It had just been a slip and there was nothing Freudian about it. Grey eyes. Not blue, like those of someone else she knew.

She swallowed convulsively and endeavoured to put Lawson Quartermain firmly out of her mind. She certainly was not enamoured with him one little piece! He could go to the devil for all she cared.

Marriage to Crispin was what she wanted. Crispin was reliable. Crispin was uncomplicated. Yes, marriage to Crispin would suit her fine. She loved him.

*   *   *

Within two months of their meeting, Felicity, Rosalinda and Jolyon had become a successful team and formed their own company, 'Ready-Made Dreams'. The name was Felicity's suggestion. She was the senior partner and had the main say in everything they did. Very soon they had employed another carpenter and seamstress, friends of Danny and Hilda, who were keen to join them.

When Lawson eventually called in at the shop he was amazed with the progress they had made and offered his congratulations. 'Do I

120

dare?' he mimicked Felicity. 'You dared all right!'

'I couldn't have done it without Rosalinda,' she said modestly. He was marvellously tanned after his American trip and oozed good health from every pore, while his cashmere sweater was the exact blue of his eyes. As he stood in a beam of spring sunshine his chestnut halo was highlighted and she had great difficulty in concentrating on what she was saying. 'I owe you a great deal for introducing her to me.'

'Only too glad to have been of assistance.'

They went into the back of the shop where Rosalinda was making tea.

'Well, what do you think of her, Lawson?' the elderly lady asked. 'Isn't she a gem?'

His eyes feasted on Felicity's warm cheeks. 'A perfect gem,' he murmured at last.

Rosalinda chuckled. 'That's not what I meant and you know it.' She adopted a stage whisper. 'I must warn you, Felicity, to be careful of him. One look from those dangerous eyes can melt the hardest heart. And yours is anything but hard.'

'Thanks. I'll try to remember that.'

Lawson grinned easily. 'I hear you're employing a staff of four now . . .'

'And that's enough,' Felicity forestalled him. 'We don't want to get too big. Small and exclusive, that's us. We're not trying to compete with the hypermarkets.'

Lawson's tone changed subtly. 'Are you

managing to keep up with the work all right? I mean, you're not having to neglect Crispin's children?'

'I'm doing fine,' she assured him, wondering why he always had to bring Crispin into the conversation and why he looked so sour when he did so.

Jolyon popped his head round the door. 'There's another load of wallpaper on a van outside. We're going to need larger premises soon.'

'Ye-es,' agreed Felicity slowly. 'But we must be careful not to overdo it. Something slightly larger would be all right as long as we keep it strictly a cottage industry.'

'I'll start looking tomorrow,' said Jolyon.

After Lawson had gone the two women got down to the book work. Both found it difficult. Felicity had never been involved in finances and Rosalinda hadn't earned enough before to have to keep complicated books.

'Lawson's a nice fellow, isn't he?' remarked Rosalinda.

'Yes,' Felicity replied without thinking. Then, 'Yes, I suppose he is. If you don't cross swords with him all the time, as I do.'

'Ah well, I speak as an older woman,' said Rosalinda. 'He won't let a younger woman get near him these days. Actresses don't count! It was different before he met Imogen. She really messed him up. No man likes to be made a fool of and she was a praying mantis.'

Felicity kept her eyes on the accounts book and pretended she knew what Rosalinda was talking about. She sensed she only had to hint she was not familiar with the details of Lawson's past and Rosalinda would shut up like the proverbial clam. She acknowledged it was a sneaky way to discover the truth but she couldn't bear not knowing about the woman who, as she had guessed all along, had hurt him and caused him to malign all women in his plays.

'He should never have had anything to do with her,' went on Rosalinda innocently. 'I was present when they announced their engagement and I had a terrible foreboding about it all.'

Felicity made out she was adding up a column of figures.'

'I mean,' said Rosalinda, 'The woman was a lot older than him for a start. She already had a kid and had left her husband for another man before Lawson came on the scene. That should have warned him. But she was so beautiful, with that hair and that skin, the kind of woman men murder for. Well, she *was* a top fashion model. He was young and I don't suppose he could help but fall. He really loved little Gregg too and would have made a wonderful father . . .'

Rosalinda stopped suddenly, aware that Felicity was listening intently. 'Oh goodness, you didn't know, did you? Me and my big mouth!'

'No, I didn't know,' admitted Felicity. 'But I suspected there was someone.' She hesitated. 'Won't you tell me the rest?'

Rosalinda shrugged. 'I might as well finish it now I've started.' She stared into space. 'Six months after their engagement Imogen left him for someone else. Lawson wouldn't accept it was over and followed them to Upton's harbour where they were about to board the other man's yacht. He pleaded with her to return to him but she just laughed in his face. They had a king-sized row.'

She gave a shiver before continuing. 'Imogen put the boy in the car and drove off to where the yacht was moored, but she was half crazy with anger. She turned too quickly and the car went off the jetty—straight into the water.'

Felicity gasped out loud. 'Oh no! How terrible for him!'

'Lawson dived in to try and rescue them but couldn't get the doors open and had to watch them drown. By the time help arrived it was too late.' Rosa Linda's voice was choked with sadness. 'Little Gregg was three years old.'

Felicity closed her eyes and pictured the scene. No wonder he had been so unreasonable when Bryony fell into the stream. He'd been through it all before and it must have evoked some bitter memories.

'Imogen was a selfish bitch,' remarked

Rosalinda vehemently. 'She held him back all the time. She wouldn't let him work. She always wanted taking here or flying there. But he adored her and danced attendance to her every whim. She was a shallow person all totally wrong for him, but you can't tell people who think they're in love. After she perished he was absolutely shattered. I thought he'd never get over it. But he did and produced his best work ever.'

'Like the two plays I've recently read,' murmured Felicity. 'Scathing towards women.'

'Yes, but with a lot of humour. And, well, he's got a point. It's what the public wants, obviously.'

'Do you think he'll get involved again?'

'Very doubtful, I should say.'

Felicity had much to think about that evening. In many ways Lawson's attitude now made sense. For instance, the way he castigated her for, as he believed, using the children to persuade Crispin to marry her. In his book she was just another scheming woman leading some poor innocent man astray. It was understandable why he flew off the handle every time Crispin's name came up. She must try to be more tolerant in future.

Poor Lawson! To love like that and then . . . Felicity felt a lump in her throat as a vision of Imogen entered her mind. A beauty, Rosalinda had said. She glanced in the mirror over the sink as she did the washing up. No chance of anyone saying that about her!

*   *   *

The partners took over a small shop in the centre of the High Street. There was a yard at the rear with a tumbledown shed and Felicity lost no time in converting it into a warehouse.

As soon as everything was ready they arranged a cheese and wine party for the press. It resulted in good publicity and more customers.

June was a month for celebrations. Troy and Bryony both had birthdays then and Felicity decided to have one big party to cover the two occasions. Each child invited six friends and, as the weather was fine, they were able to set up the table in the garden.

Several neighbours came to complain about the noise and stayed to enjoy the food and the games. Lawson also strolled over with two large boxes of chocolates.

Felicity, with hindsight, recognised the wistful way he talked to the children, and understood the heartache he had suffered when little Gregg had died. She made a silent vow she would never lose her temper with him again.

Troy had proved to be a promising table-tennis player and was entered in several tournaments, while Bryony had started tap-dancing lessons as well as ballet. Each

Saturday afternoon Felicity dispatched them to the community centre in the town while she got on with her designing.

At four o'clock she would walk to the bus-stop to collect them and, as they made their way back to the house, she heard about their latest progress.

But this Saturday only Bryony alighted from the bus.

'Where's Troy?'

'Don't know,' mumbled Bryony.

Felicity tilted the little girl's downcast chin. 'I think you do know.'

'He didn't want you to find out about . . .' Bryony's rosebud lips trembled.

'Find out? What's he done now?'

'This letter is for you.' Bryony produced a crumpled envelope from her anorak pocket. 'It's from the table-tennis man.'

Felicity ripped open the envelope and scanned the lines. 'Oh no!' Troy was accused of stealing five pounds from another boy's coat pocket. 'He doesn't need money. What's he done with the money his Daddy sent for his birthday? He has enough, more than enough! Why?'

'He's saving to get to the Gulf. He wants to see Daddy.'

Felicity sank down on to the seat in the bus shelter. 'He's a naughty boy. His father is going to be very angry with him. Have you no idea where he is?'

'He's . . . stowing away on a boat.' Bryony began to cry. 'He made me promise not to tell. Don't let him know I snitched on him.'

'Hush, darling, I shan't tell on you.' Her brain was working overtime. A boat? Was he planning to hitch-hike to the harbour at Upton St Jude? Supposing . . . 'Oh Bryony, what are we going to do?'

'Tell Lawson?' she offered hopefully.

'No, I don't think he need be involved in our troubles all the time.' Felicity was convinced this was a childish prank which would come to nothing, so was not as concerned as she might have been. After all, stowing away couldn't be very easy. Troy was bound to get caught and he would soon be home with his tail between his legs.

'We'll go and get the car and drive to Upton harbour.' After that she supposed they would have to notify the police, but she would only resort to such drastic action if all else failed. 'Come on.'

They hurried to The Old Smithy and Felicity backed the car out of the garage.

'I want to spend a penny,' said Bryony.

'Oh, hurry up, then,' sighed Felicity, letting her into the house.

Felicity returned to sit in the car, drumming her fingers on the steering-wheel and wondering why Bryony was taking so long. 'Come on,' she said again when the little girl came out. 'What are you hanging about for?'

'I've phoned Lawson,' she replied stubbornly. 'He's coming straight away.'

Felicity's heart sank. 'What did you want to do that for? I told you we didn't need him. Troy is only playing a prank.'

'We do need him. He's my friend. He saved me from the stream.'

'That has nothing to do with this,' Felicity muttered irritably. 'You talk as if he's the answer to everything, but he's only a man.'

Even as she spoke she knew he was more than that.

Bryony wasn't to be swayed so easily. 'You said he was a knight in shining armour.'

'I was kidding.' Felicity pushed the child into the rear seat and closed the door. 'Lawson is a busy man. He's fed up with getting you two out of trouble all the time. And he always blames me,' she added wryly, switching on the ignition. 'If I'm quick we can get away before he arrives.'

'Too late,' said Bryony as a white car screeched to a halt beside them.

Lawson was out and across the driveway in seconds. He placed a hand on the wound-down window of her car. 'Bryony said come quickly. What's up?'

'Nothing I can't handle,' said Felicity shortly. She put the car in gear. 'Thank you all the same.'

He kept his hand on the rim of the glass. 'Something's up,' he insisted. 'Tell me, what is it?'

'Troy's runned away,' offered Bryony.

'Bryony!' Felicity cried with exasperation. 'It's nothing to do with Mr Quartermain.'

His hand came through the window and landed on her shoulder. 'All right, I agree, it's nothing to do with me. But I'd like to help. May I?'

Put like that she didn't see how she could refuse and she switched off the engine. What an infuriating man! 'Well, Bryony thinks he's gone to stow away on a boat so I was going to drive over to the little harbour . . .'

'No need,' said Lawson. 'I know the harbourmaster. I'll ring him right away.' He cocked an eyebrow at her. 'On your phone?'

She nodded resignedly. 'Thanks.'

She stood beside him in the hall while he made the call and from his replies deduced that the harbourmaster was sending men out to scour the area right away.

Lawson replaced the receiver. 'He'll phone back when he has anything to report. Positive or negative.' His eyes studied her face. 'What made him decide to run away to sea? He won't get far without money.'

'He's got . . .' Felicity bit her lip, too ashamed to admit Troy was a thief.

Lawson watched her shrewdly. 'How much has he got?'

'A fiver Crispin sent him for his birthday and . . . another fiver.'

Bryony appeared in the kitchen doorway with a carton of ice cream she'd taken from the fridge. 'He stole it from Henry.'

Felicity said quickly, 'You don't know that for sure, there might have been a mistake.'

'No. Troy said he took it.' Bryony handed her the ice cream. 'Can I have some of this, please?'

'May I have some, please?' Lawson corrected her with a grin.

Misunderstanding him, Felicity went to the kitchen to take plates and spoons from the cabinet. The others trailed after her. As she passed a portion of ice cream to Lawson he looked surprised for a moment. 'Thank you.'

She suddenly realised the meaning of his previous remark and burst out laughing.

'That's better,' he observed. 'This may not be the tragedy we are anticipating.' He sat at the table opposite to Bryony. 'I ran away to sea when I was about his age. We were on holiday in York and I'd been reading *Mr Midshipman Easy*. A life on the ocean wave seemed very appealing so I packed my comics and a couple of bars of chocolate and set off. I was convinced I was heading for Scarborough which I knew was by the sea. When I was picked up I was in Harrogate so I was going in the opposite direction.'

Felicity watched him with her head on one side trying to see him as an eight-year-old boy with short trousers and grubby knees. She was unable to hide a grin.

'Have I said something funny?' He took a spoonful of ice-cream. 'This is good. Aren't you having any?'

'Oh, why not?' She spooned another helping on to a plate. 'I don't suppose it will make much difference to Troy's fate.'

She made a pot of tea and asked, 'Are your parents alive?'

'My father died a while back.' His tone indicated they had been close. 'My mother married again and lives in the south of France. Her husband is French and owns a vineyard. I go there sometimes to unwind.'

Felicity thought she might as well go on prying while he was in this responsive mood. 'Did you have a happy childhood?'

'Very. My parents doted on me and granted my every whim.' He winked at Bryony. 'No wonder I turned out as I badly as I did!'

'You're not bad, you're nice,' she argued.

'Thank you, my dear, for that vote of confidence.' He glanced cheekily at Felicity. 'I don't think your aunt agrees with you somehow.'

'She does,' insisted Bryony. 'She thinks you're a knight in shining armour.'

'Does she now?'

Pink-faced, Felicity said, 'Don't be silly, Bryony.'

'You did! You did!'

Felicity quickly changed the subject, 'It must

have been strange being an only child. There were five of us and it was always bedlam, having to share bedrooms and never being able to get into the bathroom.'

'You know, at school I used to envy the boys with brothers and sisters,' he replied, 'But there were compensations as I've just outlined. And it made me self-sufficient, I suppose, and content with my own company.'

She thought, he's telling me he doesn't need anyone.

'Everybody needs somebody,' she protested, unintentionally speaking her thoughts out loud.

He watched her obliquely. 'Maybe.'

Bryony dipped her finger in her ice cream and allowed Pi to lick it off. 'Did you have a cat when you were a little boy?'

'No, but I had a dog—and a pony.'

'How lovely!' Bryony looked wistful. 'Wish I could have a pony.'

'You'll have to ask Daddy when he comes home in August,' said Felicity.

'Could I? Will you 'suade him?'

'I expect so.'

'Oh, Auntie Fliss! You're wonderful!' Bryony clapped her hands. 'Isn't she wonderful, Lawson?'

'Wonderful!'

Felicity heaved a great sigh. 'Will you guys cut it out!'

They were finishing the ice cream when the

phone rang shrilly. Lawson got to it first. 'Yes, yes.' He nodded into the receiver. 'Will do. Cheers, Tom, I owe you one.'

'Well?'

'Troy's not there.'

CHAPTER EIGHT

Felicity's face drained of colour. She had been confident this was a mild misdemeanour which would soon be over, now there seemed to be more to contend with after all.

'What can have happened?'

Lawson was dialling. 'I'm calling the police.'

'Oh, yes, I suppose that's best.' She leaned despondently against the hall table. 'Thank you.'

He finished the call and said, 'They want to see you, with a recent photograph of Troy and a list of the clothes he was wearing. Would you like me to fetch Win over here to keep an eye on Bryony for you?'

She nodded and he picked up the phone again.

It started to rain, a fierce summer storm that pelted the windows and splashed noisily into the water butts, and Felicity hoped her nephew would seek shelter wherever he was.

She found a school photograph. 'He was wearing a white T-shirt with Mickey Mouse on it and blue jeans and a blue anorak and white socks and blue trainers . . .' Her voice broke.

Lawson said quickly, 'I'll come to the police station with you. We'll take my car.' He saw her hesitate and quipped, 'If you think I'm a knight in shining armour, I'd better act the part . . .' He broke off as Win arrived.

They drove in silence, the only sound the efficient swish of the windscreen wipers.

A policewoman took down a description of Troy's clothing and was confident they would find him soon. 'His distinctive blond hair will make identification easy.'

She went off to organise a search of the area and they sat on a bench to wait.

It seemed a lifetime to Felicity. Just when her spirits had sunk to their lowest depth, the policewoman returned to tell them a patrol car had found Troy.

It was a shamefaced little boy who came into the station wearing the cap of one of the constables.

Felicity had already decided he must be punished for putting everybody to so much trouble, but he was drenched to the skin and looked thoroughly miserable. She just held out her arms and he rushed into them.

'I'm sorry, Auntie Fliss. Don't tell Daddy.'

'Hush, we'll see,' she murmured. 'That was very naughty of you, you know, frightening everybody and putting the police to all this bother.'

He watched her solemnly, taking his scolding like a man.

'I'm sorry I frightened you. I didn't realise . . .'

Lawson ruffled the boy's damp blond hair. 'Of course you didn't. You were too excited to think of others. I ran away when I was your age. I'll tell you about it some day.'

'Cor!' said Troy.

'Come on then, old son,' said Lawson, 'Let's get you home. There's ice cream for supper.'

When they arrived home Win was upstairs reading a bedtime story. Assured that Troy was all right, she called, 'I'll be down in a moment.'

Felicity went straight to the fridge to get the ice cream. 'Now, Troy. I want some answers. Why did you take that money?'

'I wanted to get back at that twit Henry. He's always boasting about his parents . . . How they go everywhere together and . . .'

Felicity met Lawson's eyes across the table.

Troy went off to see his sister and Felicity said, 'We'll probably never get to the bottom of it.'

'Complex creatures, children,' said Lawson. 'Are you going to tell his father?'

'I think not. I don't want to worry him and I don't want to let Troy down. I'll have to see the table tennis people. Troy will be thrown out of the club, most likely.'

'I'll have a word with them.'

'Thank you, that would be helpful. I hope

136

the other boys won't make his life a misery.'

'Troy will probably be a hero,' Lawson muttered dryly.

They heard Win coming down the stairs and Felicity said. 'Well, thank you for everything, Lawson.'

With an easy movement, too fast to allow for any evasive action on her part, he cushioned her cheeks in his palms.

She steadied herself for the onslaught of his lips but he merely kissed her cheek then drew away. A laugh, deep and sonorous, erupted from his throat as Win came into view.

Later Felicity realised with a jolt she had wanted his kiss. And yet she was sure it would have meant nothing to him. He, who had half of the young actresses in London running after him. For a horrible moment she felt she had betrayed Crispin. She told herself firmly she would not be another of Lawson's 'groupies'. All right, she was attracted to him. Who wouldn't be! But attraction was far removed from love. She loved Crispin.

Troy was subdued for a day or two but soon became his old self again. And he wasn't asked to leave the table tennis club. Lawson had explained the situation satisfactorily, it seemed, and he was to be given another chance.

Life at The Old Smithy went on as usual, but Felicity experienced a certain restlessness she couldn't quite define. Her business was doing well, the children were behaving. And in a month or two Crispin would be home again.

For once the prospect held no thrill for her.

*   *   *

When summer arrived in all its glory, Felicity left the children in the tender care of Mrs Forester and travelled on the train to London to attend an exhibition of Japanese paints and lacquers.

She was passing a theatre when she saw posters bearing Lawson's name. *New Gambit* was the title of the play and there were various press quotes. 'I laughed and I cried', she read and 'Quartermain's jaundiced eye sees through the modern myth'. On an impulse she went in to see if there was a seat left for that evening's performance.

'You're lucky,' said the clerk. 'Someone returned a ticket for a seat in the stalls.'

Felicity went on to the exhibition where she made copious notes, but her mind wasn't fully on her work. All the time lurking in her brain was the tantalising thought of the forthcoming performance.

As the theatre filled up a buzz of excited anticipation ran through the audience, to fade to a hushed silence as the curtain was raised. The play was the kind of thing she had come to expect from Lawson Quartermain—caustic, humorous and highly critical of women. She loved every moment of it!

She visited the bar during the interval and noticed Vera Valance sitting on a stool by the counter, apparently alone.

Felicity smiled. 'It's well attended, isn't it?' she remarked, clutching her gin and tonic tightly as she was jostled by the crowd.

'It was bound to be.' Vera languidly sipped her drink. 'The successful formula. Can't fail.'

'Is it the first time you've seen it?' Felicity asked politely.

'Lord, no, I often pop in. Just in case Lawson happens to be here . . .' Vera stopped and looked uncomfortable. She took several little sips from her glass. 'You must think I'm crazy, hanging around Lawson all the time. At my age! I have no shame, you see.'

'Why, no, of course I don't think . . .'

'If only he'd give me a chance!' Vera's words were slurred and she had plainly had several drinks too many. 'Instead of handing all his favours to that . . . that Kiki Dawn!'

Felicity swallowed hard. She wasn't interested in Lawson in the slightest, but the thought of his handing out favours inexplicably depressed her.

'I'm not finished as an actress,' went on Vera. 'Just because he thinks I'm over the hill it doesn't mean I am. There's a lot of wear in the old girl still . . .'

Felicity realised that when Vera had referred to favours she was talking about acting parts. Her relief was very sweet.

'Why, I'm only . . . twenty-seven.' Vera's glance defied Felicity to contradict her. 'That's not past it, is it?'

Felicity, twenty-five, grinned. 'I should hope not.'

'If I could only make him see.' Vera looked across the bar and gave a nervous start. 'Why, there he is!'

Felicity followed her gaze and saw him framed in the doorway.

Vera slid off the stool unsteadily. 'Lawson!'

He didn't seem to hear her, above the din. He merely glanced around briefly then left.

Vera struggled vainly through the crowd, like a fish swimming against the tide. Then the bell rang for the second act and she was forced to give up the chase in the general exit. She looked near to tears.

With a pang of sympathy for the woman and a certain amount of anger for Lawson, Felicity returned to her seat.

An hour later she was leaving the theatre when Lawson grabbed her arm.

'Felicity! How nice to see you! You should have let me know you were coming. I would have got you a complimentary ticket.'

'I didn't know myself,' she said coldly, remembering Vera. 'How did you know I was here?'

'I saw you in the bar.'

'I was talking to Vera Valance. Didn't you

140

see her?'

He grimaced. 'I saw her!'

'Poor woman. She wanted to speak to you desperately.'

'I know. But it's the same old story every time. Frankly she's beginning to bore me.'

'That's unkind.'

'It's not unkind. She was a great actress once but she's let herself slip. Too much gin and not enough sleep. There's nothing I can do for her till she pulls herself together. I've told her so over and over.'

'I'm glad I don't have to beg to you for my living,' Felicity retorted.

'Ah, now that would be something!' He tucked her arm under his. 'And what did you think of the play?'

'I enjoyed it very much. Although I think you are most unfair to women. We're not all so predatory, you know.'

'Is that a fact?' The blue eyes glittered. 'In my experience women go all out for what they want. Take yourself, for instance. You want Crispin and . . .'

She was determined not to lose her temper with him. 'You've got it all wrong, you know. I want the children. Crispin comes with the package.'

'Really.'

She knew he was never going to believe her. 'I'd better get moving if I'm going to catch the last train.'

A devilish grin spread over his face. It reminded her of Troy when he was planning some mischief.

He waved a taxi down. 'I'll take you to the station.'

She surmised that meant he wasn't returning to Upton that night and she was glad. A long train journey with him might be overwhelming. Besides which there would have been the difficult business of getting rid of him the other end!

At the station he insisted on walking the length of the platform with her.

'The train is due to leave in three minutes,' she said, her voice loaded with exasperation. 'You needn't have come on the platform. I'm not an idiot.'

'Ah, but it gives me the opportunity to kiss you goodbye in the time-honoured fashion.' He glanced round at several couples in passionate embraces. 'It's what stations are for.'

'Oh . . .'

For a breathless moment she waited, then his arms were about her, his mouth hard on hers. As his strong body pressed against her, a wave of euphoria swept away her reservations. Slowly but surely her hands crept round his waist and she was holding on for dear life, her own lips matching the hunger of his kiss. Starved of love as she was, and sometimes wondering if she would ever win the man of her dreams, Lawson's interest boosted her confidence. The kiss went on—and on—till she lost all sense of time and place.

Doors slammed along the platform. Lawson's grip slackened and she leaned drunkenly against him, her head reeling. 'I wish you hadn't done that,' she murmured.

'Do you?' he enquired silkily. 'Do you really?'

There came a strident whistle and she broke away to board the train. She had settled in a seat in an open compartment when she was aware he was also on the train.

'What . . .? I thought . . .' she stammered as he took the seat opposite. 'You said you weren't travelling back to Upton St Jude.'

'No, you assumed that.'

She felt her cheeks burn. 'You purposely let me think it was the case. You knew what I assumed and didn't correct me.'

'True. You wouldn't have let me kiss you if you'd known.' He gave her a wicked smile. 'Now, would you?'

She deliberately took a paperback from her tote-bag. As she found her page she heard him laugh softly.

It was a good twenty minutes before she realised she wasn't taking in one word of what she was reading. Her mind was filled with the memory of his lips on hers. She sneaked a look at him over the top of the page and saw he had closed his eyes and was dozing.

Her brain was far too active for her to doze too so she seized this opportunity to watch him unobserved, wondering what it was about him that made him so attractive. His features were quite ordinary taken singly. It was when viewed as a whole his looks became dangerous. This conclusion sent a spasm of excitement zigzagging down her spine. His clothes were casual, a long-sleeved poplin shirt, the colour of autumn bracken, tucked into cream-coloured slacks with a lightweight matching jacket in the rack above, and brown moccasins. Deceptively simple, but to her trained eye, expensively cut, demonstrating breeding and good taste.

Darn him! she thought. Why doesn't he leave me alone? Why does he insist on playing with my emotions all the time? He has no intention of getting deeply involved with a woman again, and knows I'm not interested in him. So why?

All at once she thought she knew. It was to save Crispin from falling into her clutches. At first glance it appeared ridiculous but the more she considered it the more feasible it became. Lawson had set himself up as judge and jury to condemn the fickleness of women. Why shouldn't he go out of his way to preserve one of his sex from a self-confessed schemer? By 'messing her about' and trying to make her fall for him he was at least giving Crispin a chance to escape.

She must have dozed after all for the next thing she knew they were pulling into the station.

Lawson put a hand on her knee. 'Come on, sleeping beauty.' He put on his jacket. 'I've got the car in the station car park. I'll give you a lift home.'

She didn't see how she could get out of it, so saved her breath and followed him to the car park.

As they travelled long the High Street Felicity asked Lawson to drive slowly past 'Ready-Made Dreams' so she could view Rosalinda's new display. Their latest line was nursery-rhyme furniture—a Wee Willie Winkie bed, a Little Jack Horner corner unit and Humpty Dumpty chairs. Rosalinda had dressed models to demonstrate the pieces and the effect was eye-catching.

Moments later the car swept in through the main entrance of the estate and came to a halt beside the kissing-gate.

Felicity undid her seat-belt and Lawson leaned across her to open the door for her. As the interior light came on she felt uneasy.

Here was that moment she had been dreading, saying goodnight to him, not knowing what he expected of her—but having a good idea! A delicate situation at the best of times and one for which there seemed no rules. More worldly women than her must have wondered whether to submit to an unwelcome kiss or risk the chance of being thought ungrateful. She didn't want him to kiss her, it only caused confusion. But then, that was his intention, she reasoned.

'Thank you for the lift,' she said primly. 'I know what you're up to, you know.'

'Do you indeed? And what is that, pray?'

'You're trying to make me . . . You think that if I . . .' Help! Why had she started this? 'Anyway, I'd be obliged if you didn't kiss me again.'

Almost reflectively, he murmured, 'I shouldn't have kissed you in the first place . . .' He stopped and cleared his throat self-consciously. When he continued the sardonic tone was back. 'I'm sorry to disappoint you, but I have no intention of kissing you again. You'll just have to stew.'

She might have known he'd say something like that but she'd asked for it with her stupid remarks. She scrambled out of the car. 'Of all the conceited, arrogant, self-satisfied . . .' She ran out of adjectives.

'You forgot smug,' he offered, making no attempt to follow her. 'And swollen-headed. Then there's bumptious. I like bumptious best . . .'

'Oh, shut up!' And she bolted along the path to The Old Smithy.

He shouldn't have kissed her at the station, she fumed. And she shouldn't have let him! It complicated things. She hadn't thought of him

146

in that way before. Not really. Well, maybe a little, but not for *real*. Now . . .

She shook the bewitchment away. This was crazy! She must be going out of her mind! He was the last person . . .

*   *   *

Somewhere in a bright place, even brighter lights were exploding in Felicity's brain. And there was a heavy rock beat, making her head throb. She was standing on a draughty platform and Lawson was kissing her lips, her eyes, her throat.

She woke up with a start and dragged herself into the bathroom.

Her eyes in the mirror looked puffy and she had a high colour. She took a shower, forcing her mind off Lawson and mentally planned her day. The children had broken up from school and she would take them to the library for fairy-story readings; drop in at the shop to see if Rosalinda wanted anything; work on a new design.

The trouble was, she realised as she stared at the blank paper on her drawing-board, she was stuck for an idea. It was nothing new. Sometimes she would sit there for hours, despairing of ever coming up with an original thought. Even though past experience told her the mental block would pass, she always suspected the worst.

When she returned to collect the children, the junior librarian was just finishing a Brothers Grimm story and on the blackboard was an illustration of the interior of a cottage. The old-fashioned furniture was thick and clumsy-looking, painted in garish colours, the type produced in Holland centuries ago. *Hindenloopen* she thought it was called.

Felicity's brain churned into action.

She signalled to the children to wait for her and sped upstairs to the craft section, descending half an hour later, her arms laden with books on Dutch furniture.

For a week she studied and sketched late into the night but still couldn't get the design exactly as she wanted it. It had to be original but look authentic, a pattern which could be fretworked on the backs of the chairs and repeated on the soft furnishings.

She was staring vacantly out of the window when Crispin telephoned from the Gulf. He sounded unusually cheerful and his words tumbled over each other in his excitement.

'Dearest Felicity. I'll be home for the August holiday and then . . . I've got something to . . . No, I mustn't jump the gun and spoil my surprise. But, oh Felicity, I feel wonderful. I thought over what you said at Easter and you're absolutely right. I've been so blind insisting I . . .'

'What is it, Crispin? Please tell me.'

'No,' he replied firmly, 'I won't even hint at

148

it, but I know everything is going to work out fine for us. The answer seems so simple now. You must think I'm an idiot rambling on like this but . . . I can't wait to see you and the children. I'd better ring off now before I make a fool of myself. 'Bye, dear.'

She replaced the receiver, letting the implications sink in. Crispin was coming home to propose! It was what she had longed for. Crispin and the children—her own ready-made family. And more children of her own in time.

She sat on the patio and sifted through plans for the future. Would they live here or in the Gulf? He had once mentioned applying for a transfer to Britain. With her kind of work she could reside anywhere, but it would be hard giving up the shop. And yet . . . it might be exciting living abroad. She could collect Far-Eastern designs, those wonderful carpets and ceramics, and open another shop somewhere. She was adaptable. Wherever Crispin chose to live would suit her.

*　　　*　　　*

Felicity drove the children to the table-tennis club barbecue and arranged to collect them at five. A whole day to herself!

On her return home she flipped through her sketch-books to see if there was anything she could use as a starting-point for the design she was seeking. And all at once she found it. The rough sketch of the Quartermain coat-of-arms. The swan and stork, necks entwined, on the wrought-iron gate leading to the walled rose garden. A shivery sensation told her she was on the right track. She must go to the manor at once.

Reluctant to risk bumping into Lawson, she phoned Win who assured her he had just gone out and wasn't expected back till five.

The housekeeper, green hat still in place, was baking when Felicity arrived and the aroma of fresh scones filled the kitchen.

Felicity made her way to the walled garden and let herself through the wrought-iron gate to where the old roses were in full bloom, a riot of colour and reeking with perfume.

Sitting on a grassy knoll, her sketch pad on her knees, she worked steadily, making sketch after sketch and losing all track of time. It was hot but, in her halter-neck top and cotton skirt, the sun didn't bother her. She tanned easily and her skin was already bronzed.

Presently she heard a distant church clock striking four and returned to the kitchen to say goodbye.

'Lawson's kept the gardens as near to the original as possible,' she remarked. 'I like that.' She added wistfully. 'He promised to show me over the house one day.'

Win smiled knowingly. 'Why don't I show you round?'

150

'I've got to collect the children at five . . . and I don't want to bump into Lawson.'

'Heaps of time.'

Felicity deposited her things on the kitchen table and followed Win out into the hall. They ascended the elegant stone staircase, its fleur-de-lys carpet and tapestry-hung walls in keeping with the great age of the house.

Win opened the first door on the landing. 'This is the only room he's done upstairs. It's his.'

The paintwork was white with bronze embellishments, and gold brocade curtains fell gracefully from ceiling to floor. There was a four-poster bed with velvety drapes, a rosewood writing-desk and a set of button-back chairs. The only sign of the twentieth century was an array of men's toiletries on the chest of drawers.

There were four more bedrooms on this floor, each with its own dressing-room, but they had been sadly neglected and there was a dank smell. Before any more restoration work could be attempted the wall-paper would have to be removed and the bare floors treated for woodworm and dry rot.

The curtains were very old and almost disintegrated in her hands. They needed to be replaced, as did the chair covers, but the rest—the day-bed covers, dressing chest sets and cushions—could be successfully repaired.

She recalled Lawson's invitation to help

restore these rooms and knew she would have derived immense satisfaction from undertaking the work. Studying old books to get the style right, scouring the county for the wood and fabrics, designing the skirting-boards and new curtains. One of her carpenters could have been employed on the replacement work, under her guidance. The repairs she would have done herself, lovingly, by hand.

'There's another room up in the tower,' said Win. 'I clean it once a month but he keeps it locked, because there's some valuable stuff there. It's supposed to be haunted. I wish I could show you but he keeps the key.'

'Never mind. Another time . . .' Felicity heard a car outside and, gazing from the nearest window, saw the Lotus Turbo sweep into the courtyard. 'Oh no!' She grimaced. 'I'd better scoot. You keep him talking and I'll sneak out.'

'Don't you think you're overdoing it?' asked Win sarcastically. 'He won't eat you.'

'Can I have that in writing?'

Win shrugged. 'Rightio, we'll do it your way.'

Felicity stood on the landing and watched through the ornate balustrade as Win descended the stairs.

At the bottom she met Lawson.

'Is that Felicity's sketch book in the kitchen?' he asked abruptly. 'Has she been here?'

'Yes . . . er . . . she must have left it . . .'

His suspicious eyes looked sharply up the stairs.

Felicity dodged back but was too late. He'd seen her. In a moment he had bounded, two at a time, up the stairs.

CHAPTER NINE

Lawson treated Felicity to one of his penetrating stares. He wore an open-necked azure shirt with stone-washed jeans and his hair was dishevelled as if he had driven with the top down. 'Make yourself at home!' he muttered sarcastically.

She refused to be intimidated and said pertly, 'You once promised I could look over the house, remember?'

'I do. But I had rather hoped I would be the one to show you round.'

She made as if to pass him. 'I have to collect the children.'

'So soon?' He raised his dark brows. 'Troy told me the barbecue wasn't finishing till five.'

She wondered whose side those children were on.

'Has Win shown you everything? What's your verdict?'

'You've worked wonders.' Her voice softened. 'It must have cost a fortune to have

153

got so far.'

'An arm and a leg. As a matter of fact the work kept me sane after . . . a personal tragedy.'

She nodded compassionately.

'Have you seen the haunted tower?'

'No. Win mentioned it but said you had the key.'

He went into his bedroom for a moment to reappear with a chatelaine of huge iron keys. 'Follow me,' he commanded and his long legs carried him along the landing and up a spiral flight of stone steps to a stout oak door.

Felicity caught her breath with sheer delight as she entered the circular room where the furniture was of another time. The washing-stand was made of pine and marble, the dressing-cupboard of ebony. Dominating everything was a vast four-poster bed, its faded canopy and counterpane bearing the swan and stork crest embroidered in gold.

She reverently touched a wicker casket here, a silver candlestick there. 'It's truly magnificent,' she breathed.

He noted her reaction with satisfaction. 'Legend has it a female ancestor of mine was incarcerated here to prevent her from following her lover to France. They say she still haunts the place.'

'Troy would like to hear that story.' She turned slowly round. 'Restoring this room would be fascinating.'

'The job's still yours if you want it.'

'No, I'm sorry. I don't know if I'll still be living here after my marriage.' Well, he had to know sooner or later.

'You mean Crispin's actually proposed?'

'As good as.'

His brows met angrily. 'So, you've got your way, you little schemer!' In a second his humour had turned from fair to foul. 'You women! Is there anything you won't do?'

She meant to keep her temper and met his eyes evenly. 'I'm going to marry him, whether you approve or not.'

Her reply only served to inflame him further. 'You know darned well I don't approve! The poor sap didn't stand a chance. I'm sick and tired of seeing decent guys being manipulated by unscrupulous women.'

'I'd better go.'

'Yes, run along and collect his children.' He caught her wrists. 'I've told you before, you really shouldn't use those innocent children to further your own ends, you know!'

She tried to free herself but his fingers dug in deep. 'What's it got to do with you anyway?'

'I know what it's like. A woman like you . . .'

'A woman like me?' she echoed.

'. . . can wreak havoc on a man and he'll never know what's hit him.'

'Well, really!' Her temper was mounting, despite her resolve. 'Will you please let me go. You're hurting me.'

His grip relaxed a little. 'You're all the same. Out for what you can get. Cheats, the lot of you.'

He pulled her roughly towards him and his eyes, two pinpoints of blue flame, bored into her. His breath was hot on her cheek. The thought crossed her mind that he meant to punish her, though goodness knew what it had to do with him. She waited breathlessly, ready to retaliate if the need arose.

She had no idea how long they stood there, like two animals at bay, when gradually, subtly, his expression changed. The angry-eyed glint was replaced by a glazed look. He had the appearance of a man who had set out to prove he was in total control of his emotions—and failed miserably.

As the tension became unbearable, he dragged her into his arms. Her lips parted in a gasp of surprise and his ravaging mouth came down on hers like a hawk swooping on a defenceless rabbit. His kiss contained a brutal passion, igniting in her a surge of rebellion which curled through her bloodstream in a relentless tide.

All her senses were outraged. She attempted to break away from him but, wriggle as she might, there was no escape. Her mind was a ragbag of indignation. How dared he! Just wait till he'd finished, she'd . . . she'd kill him!

Then, quite suddenly, her opposition

melted. With the increased pressure of his lips, she detected a sensuous throb deep within the kernel of her womanhood. It radiated to her nerve-ends and exploded in a sunburst of desire. She closed her eyes and surrendered unconditionally to the rapture of his embrace.

'Felicity,' he whispered, his voice soft and low.

Gently he cradled the back of her head in his hands and eased her towards him once more. This kiss was as tender as the previous one had been violent. As she received the full benediction of his lips, a slumbering part of her psyche awoke. The world retreated and all she knew was the closeness of his body, the feel of his mouth on hers and a raw yearning which demanded gratification.

As she came up for air, he touched her tight curls, looping the tendrils round his finger.

She in turn tangled her hand in his wild mop of hair, then traced the contours of his face, the gaunt cheeks and the outline of his lips.

He kissed her again, whispering muffled endearments. She made no attempt to stop him when he undid the ties of her halter-top and pulled the garment down. As his hands caressed her tender flesh, she cried out with ecstasy.

He pushed her gently back on to the counterpane. She stretched out her arms to him invitingly. His eyes feasted on her semi-nakedness then he lowered his head to trail his mouth over the places his hands and eyes had touched.

'Fliss!'

He'd not called her that before. She liked it. It was the name the children used.

The children! Crispin! She groaned. Oh no!

Pushing against Lawson's shoulders, she gasped. 'Stop! Wait a minute . . . ! Please . . .'

He took no notice.

'Lawson, no!' she cried. 'I can't . . .'

He raised his head and stared disbelievingly, then he let her go and rolled away to sit on the edge of the bed.

Her body ached with unfulfilled promises. 'I'm sorry.'

He stood up and his eyes were laced with contempt. 'And you're the girl who's going to marry Crispin.' He spat out the words. 'Heaven help him!'

She recoiled as from a poisonous snake and shame poured over her. As a sob broke from her lips the need to put the blame on him was uppermost in her mind.

She jumped from the bed and ran to the door, pulling her halter into place. 'I told you before, I know why you're doing this to me. You think you'll make me fall for you and let Crispin go. Well, I won't! I . . . love him!'

He looked first stunned and then angry. When he spoke his tone was arrogant. 'How very astute of you! That was exactly my intention.'

158

His words cut her like a knife and she hit back, 'It won't make any difference. I'm going to marry Crispin.'

She darted from the room.

Win, shelling peas, looked up as Felicity raced through, snatching up her sketch book as she went.

'What the . . . ?'

'Don't ask!'

Driving to the barbecue Felicity wondered what stupidity had impelled her to go to the manor. She knew the kind of man Lawson Quartermain was, knew the motives he had for misusing her. Why hadn't she recognised the danger?

Presently cartwheels of guilt began churning through her conscience. Lawson wasn't totally to blame for her humiliation. She had gone along quite willingly with his lovemaking, wanted him to do what he had done—and more! All thoughts of her impending marriage to Crispin had been buried under the avalanche of her desire.

It wasn't until the evening when she sat on the patio with her bedtime coffee that the truth finally dawned. For a while she refused to believe it. But there was only so far she could go in falsifying her emotions.

She was in love with Lawson Quartermain.

There, she'd admitted it. Was it a new emotion, or had it been festering from the time they had met? Earlier perhaps. Hadn't she been a little in love with the intriguing picture her aunt had painted of him? She had sensed the chemistry activated between them that first day on the croquet lawn and ever since it had simply run amok.

How could life be so wicked? She didn't even like him! A man like that, who would trifle with her affections as readily as he would order another cup of tea. A man who had half the actresses of London grovelling at his feet. A man who had been made a fool of by one clever, scheming woman and now saw them all as predators.

This then was love, she thought, wretchedly. All that other nonsense she had conjured up regarding herself and Crispin now seemed ludicrous. Love had nothing to do with logic, it concerned the senses, a gut feeling that cut through pretence and revealed the truth, no matter how sour and unpalatable. Love was relentless. Love wouldn't go away. Love hurt.

Her plans for the immediate future were of paramount importance. Crispin was coming home to propose. And she would accept him— because of the children. They could move away from here and she need never see Lawson again. In time she would forget him. Crispin would never know. She would make him happy. It was her destiny.

Her shoulders dropped. Forget Lawson? She might as well try to forget her own name.

*　　　*　　　*

Troy, who had been keeping watch by the window, whooped for joy as the taxi drew up outside. 'It's Daddy!'

Felicity followed the children outside allowing them as always to greet their father first.

When she joined them they were clinging to Crispin's waist. Beside them stood a young woman, a little older than Felicity, with long blonde hair hanging down her back like a silken curtain.

'You've probably guessed my surprise. Felicity.' Crispin hugged her, as he'd done many times before. 'This is Gabriella. We're to be married.'

*　　　*　　　*

Crispin had reserved accommodation at The Swan for him and his fiancée and they had taken the children there for dinner. They had begged Felicity to accompany them, but she had declined. Her reasons were twofold. The children needed to get to know Gabriella without Felicity's influence standing in the way. And she was going to lose them, so she might as well get used to the idea.

She would have made a poor companion in any case. She was drained of all emotion. At the first opportunity she had escaped to her

161

room to weigh up this heartbreaking turn of events. Her worst fears had been realised and she was devastated but, always having despised weepy women, she had vowed she would not cry.

Gabriella was an oilman's widow whom Crispin had met in Aden. She was warm and friendly, the perfect match for him. Felicity couldn't have disliked her if she'd tried.

Plans were under way for a September wedding in Yorkshire where Gabriella's parents lived. Crispin had already applied for a transfer and intended buying a house in the same village.

He'd been gentle with Felicity, knowing how much she loved his children and would suffer after they had gone, but it didn't alter the fact that they *were* going.

She had to be strong now, for their sakes as well as her own. They were bound to be confused at a further upheaval in their young lives and it was up to her to put on a brave face and show them it was the best thing that could have happened. And it was! They would be a complete family with two parents who loved each other. She could see all too clearly now that had she married Crispin it would not have worked. Because she didn't love him. Never had.

After he brought the children home and put them to bed he had one last favour to ask of her.

'Speak to the children, will you? Explain to them why I'm uprooting them yet again. It seems an awful imposition, I know . . .'

She blinked rapidly. His unexpected request was like a final turn of the screw in her heart. 'Leave it to me.'

'Bless you, my dear.'

She took them for a last walk by the stream.

'Are you coming to Yorkshire with us, Aunty Fliss?' asked Bryony, 'I don't want to go without you. I love you.'

'And I love you both, very very much.' Felicity strove for normality in her voice. 'But you're going to have a new mummy. If I came I'd only be in the way.'

'I'll stay with you then.' The little girl's chin quivered. 'I don't want to leave here.'

'Listen, lovey, you're going to have a great life in Yorkshire. Daddy will be home all the time and your new mummy is really sweet and kind. She'll make you and Daddy very happy. He deserves to be happy again, doesn't he? You don't want him to be sad forever.'

Troy said, 'Can we come and visit you?'

'Of course. You can spend holidays here if you like.'

She went to the station to see them off and hugged them in turn, careful not to show too much emotion. They would be all right, she thought, watching the train disappear from sight. They had resented living in Upton at first, but they had adapted. Children did.

163

She wasn't so sure about herself.

She began sleeping badly but Dr Freedman refused to give her any tablets.

'There's no medical cure for your problem, I'm afraid,' he said kindly, understanding more than she gave him credit for. 'It's a cliché, I know, but time is the great healer.'

*   *   *

Felicity wandered aimlessly through the silent house. It was two weeks now since the children had left and she missed them dreadfully.

There was no escape from her poignant memories. She had kept the bedrooms exactly as they had left them. Their drawings were still pinned to the walls and in Bryony's room Pi was curled up on the fairytale duvet, his head on a jersey the little girl had outgrown.

Felicity bent to fondle the cat's ears. 'You miss them too, don't you?'

Her lips quivered and she felt stifled. She opened the window, but it didn't help. It was no good trying to behave as if nothing had changed. Everything had changed. Her dreams were in ruins.

The tears she had managed to keep at bay for so long rose to the surface and she collapsed into a chair to sob until she ached.

She couldn't go on like this, she thought as the weeping subsided. She had to pull herself together.

Perhaps it would be better to move away. But she loved the old house. And there was the shop to think about. Rosalinda and Jolyon were good friends and she couldn't let them and the carpenters down. The business was doing well and it would be foolish to give up now.

Then there was Lawson. She hadn't seen him since . . . that day, apart from the odd glimpse as the Lotus drove in and out of the gates. Win said he was writing a new play and had gone to Paris to do some research.

Felicity liked to know what he was doing. It was ridiculous she knew, but she had a strong urge to feel him near. Where was that level-headed young woman, she wondered, who had known exactly where she was going, who could take men or leave them alone?

She had tried to forget him but constantly at the back of her mind was the recollection of that afternoon in the haunted tower when he had reminded her she was a sensuous woman, conscious of her body and its needs, that ecstatic moment when his hard body had pressed against hers, his lips had kissed her lips. He had touched her intimately and for a brief moment she had been transported to paradise . . .

She stopped kidding herself. He was the reason she wouldn't be leaving. Living here, loving him as she did, would be purgatory. But leaving would be infinitely worse.

With a long-drawn-out sigh, she rose from the chair. It was beginning to get dark now. She put the light on and crossed the room to close the window.

It was then she noticed the object of her recent heartsearching coming along the path. He wore a black anorak and walked purposefully as if he meant business.

She glanced in the mirror and groaned at her reflection. Crying always left her cheeks blotchy, her eyelids swollen and her hair bedraggled. She didn't want him to see her like this. Why had she turned on the light? She could have pretended she was out.

She went downstairs as the bell rang impatiently. She wouldn't answer it.

He rattled the letter box. 'Felicity! I know you're in there.'

She opened the door six inches. 'I can't see you now...'

She started to close it again but he held it open with his foot. 'Felicity...' The deep cadence of his voice thrilled her as before.

She put the hall light on. 'I thought you were in Paris.'

'I returned early. I couldn't concentrate.' He pushed the door wide. 'I know how upset you must be at losing the children. I came to see if you were all right.' He stared hard. 'Apparently you're not.'

'Oh, this?' She dabbed at her eyes with a screwed up ball of sodden handkerchief. 'I

166

must be getting a cold.' She averted her face, envying women who managed to look lovely when they wept. She guessed Kiki Dawn would cry magnificently. 'Shouldn't you be worrying about Kiki instead of me?'

'Kiki?' He gave a short laugh. 'Kiki is secretly married to a pop-singer. They have to keep it quiet or he'll lose his young fans. She was strictly business, but she won't be hanging around here any longer. I've helped her all I can and she's on her own now.'

'I see.' The relief threatened to engulf her.

'Look, do you mind if I come in?'

She hesitated then stood aside.

He closed the door behind him and raised his hand to ruffle her mussed hair in the same way he had ruffled the children's. 'How are you?'

Feeling more tears unshed behind her lashes, she sprang away from him and hastily gathered her defences. 'Is it any of your business? Why can't you leave me alone? I don't want your pity. I just want . . .' The tears overspilled.

'Darling! Come here!' He pulled her into his arms and his mouth closed fiercely over hers.

She struggled against him. 'You beast! What satisfaction do you derive from reducing me to a pulp? Your ego must be very fragile to have to keep boosting it in such a low-down way.' She took a deep breath and shouted. 'Can't you see I love you!'

167

She shivered. Was she mad? Confessing her love to a man who would surely take advantage of her for his own amusement?

He caught his breath sharply. 'And can't you see I love you!' he shouted back.

'Why . . . what?'

Blue eyes burned into her. 'You heard me!' His lips found the edge of her eyebrow, the hollow of her throat, the line of her jaw. 'I've loved you since the moment we met. No, before then. I fell in love with the woman your aunt used to talk about. I didn't know it then but it accounts for everything, including why I tried to stop you living here.'

He rocked her gently. 'I didn't want to be dependent on a woman again, you see. I couldn't trust myself not to fall. I've been fighting my instincts all these months, but it's no good. I admit defeat.'

Slowly the significance of his words sank in. A delicious feeling of well-being crept over her and she savoured the physical bond blossoming between them.

His next kiss had her lungs begging for mercy and little eddies of erotic current threatened to knock her feet from under her.

He held her at arm's length. 'You were so enamoured with Crispin you didn't notice me . . .'

She stroked his angular cheek. 'Oh, didn't I?'

'At first I was only interested in stopping you

from marrying Crispin,' he reflected, 'Because he's a nice guy and I didn't want you to get away with your scheming. I didn't realise my motives were more personal than that.'

'I didn't love Crispin,' she told him. 'It was as I said all along. I just wanted the children.'

He hugged her tight. 'Well, that's a relief.'

'Oh Lawson!' Her voice expressed the desire leaping within her and there came an answering murmur from deep in his throat.

He strung a row of kisses along her brow and his hands were everywhere. 'We have some unfinished business to attend to,' he whispered.

She thought of the fire he had kindled in her before. Wanting him, needing him, she nodded wordlessly.

Hand in hand they sped up the stairs.

The night was filled with a savage passion that she would not have not believed possible. He claimed her utterly and completely as she had known he would, and all she could do was cling to the source of the storm raging about her till they merged into one being. He was in turn forceful and tender and they soared to the heights of ecstasy before their hunger was spent.

Felicity awoke to find a pink dawn beyond the window and Lawson, wearing just his jeans, carrying a loaded tray and followed by Pi.

She wriggled to a sitting position as the cat jumped on to the duvet. 'Breakfast in bed?

This is nice.'

'Don't expect it every day after we're married.'

She choked on the coffee and put the cup down. 'Married? You're that serious?' she teased, still in shock from the rapid reversal of her fortunes.

He shrugged his bare shoulders negligently and fondled the cat. 'Well, we might as well.'

He appeared to be at a loss for more words and she viewed him with awe. Lawson Quartermain struggling for something to say was a rare sight indeed.

His hand gripped her chin and tilted her head so that she had to look at him, while his thumb caressed her lips.

'Marry me, Felicity!' Those amazingly blue eyes that plagued all her sleeping hours were filled with anxiety and she relished the power she had over him.

'Have you thought what this will do to your image?' she enquired, prolonging his agony. 'To Lawson Quartermain, the man who hates women?'

'Time for a new image. The man who loves women! One woman, very much, as my current play will show. Oh Felicity, I've waited for you all my life. This is a big step for me. I've been wary of women since . . .'

She said gently, 'I know about Imogen.'

He touched her cheek. 'I hadn't a clue what love was till I met you. I thought I could get you out of my system with a few kisses, but it only made matters worse. I've been through hell.'

'Hm! I know the feeling.'

'You don't need a ready-made family.' He kissed the tip of her nose. 'We'll start our own. And between us we'll restore the manor to its former glory.'

'Could we?' She grinned up at him. 'I'd like that.'

'Does that mean "yes"?'

'Darling Lawson! As if you didn't know!'

They made plans as they breakfasted. To Spain first so that Lawson could meet her parents, and a Christmas wedding.

By the time the birds were up and singing, Felicity had decided dreams were all right—for Sleeping Beauty. But she was awake now and ready for what her aunt would have called her destiny.

What a passionate awakening it had been!

We hope you have enjoyed this Large Print book. Other Chivers Press or G.K. Hall & Co. Large Print books are available at your library or directly from the publishers.

For more information about current and forthcoming titles, please call or write, without obligation, to:

Chivers Press Limited
Windsor Bridge Road
Bath BA2 3AX
England
Tel. (01225) 335336

OR

G.K. Hall & Co.
P.O. Box 159
Thorndike, Maine 04986
USA
Tel. (800) 223-2336

All our Large Print titles are designed for easy reading, and all our books are made to last.